SUGAR: AN EVE'S FURY MC NOVEL

RAE B. LAKE

EVE'S FURY
MC CLUB

PROLOGUE

It's been two hours since Glenn has started crying. He's got colic, and most of the women in here don't have children.

"I don't know what I should be doing. I did everything that the doctor said. What do I need to do?" Addison rakes her hand through her hair.

"It's because he can feel how upset you are. Go on in the room, and I'll take care of the baby."

The relief is visible on her face, and I can see that she is only seconds from having a breakdown.

"Are you sure? I mean, I don't want...." She wrings her hands after I take Glenn away from her.

"Addison, go get some rest. I'll be fine." I smile at her and then focus all my attention on the baby. He squirms around in my arms, and I take my time rocking him back and forth.

"Oh, little boy, you hurting?" I speak to him in my best

baby voice. The one that I had perfected since I was a little child and would pretend my dolls were real.

A voice that I will never get to use on my own child because Baxter made sure that I'd never get pregnant.

I bounce Glenn up and down and side to side, soothing him with my presence and my voice. I sing my favorite nursery rhymes, and soon little Glenn is falling fast asleep.

When he is finally down, I lay him in the bassinet that Addison keeps in the main room.

"You're really good with him."

I twirl around and slam my hand to my chest in fright, "Oh sweetheart, you nearly killed me." I do my best not to show him how anxious I am.

"I'm sorry, I didn't mean to sneak up on you.Thought I could help with the baby, but you seem to have it all under control." Jag leans against the door frame.

"Yeah, Addison would have been able to handle it, but she was a little overwhelmed. I smile at him and wait for whatever else he has to say. Jag never engages with anyone unless he has something profound to say. "I'm happy to help."

"You know you're family, right?"

Here it is.

"Yeah, of course. Why would you say that?" I scratch the back of my neck and look back to where the baby is still sound asleep.

"No reason, just seems like you're holding back a bit. I want you to know that you don't have to." Jag shrugs but doesn't wait for me to reply.

I hate that he always seems to see things that everyone

misses. That he always finds a way to dig out secrets that are best left buried.

There are some things that people shouldn't know, and who I really am is one of them.

I love every one of the girls in this club, but if anyone found out who I was, it'd be a mess. They'd never understand how I could just leave everything I had before to be here with nothing. It's not easy trying to hide the fact that I was once semi-famous. Almost famous and completely unhappy.

I think back on Baxter and what our relationship was like. Pure horror is all I see when I remember him. A man everyone wanted to be around on the outside but a devil on the inside.

I do my best to push those bad memories out of my mind. I walk over to Addison's room to let her know the baby is finally asleep.

"Really? Oh, thank you so much." She wipes a hand under her eyes and pulls me into a big hug.

"Oh, honey, don't worry about it. You know I'd do anything for that little one and you too." I kiss her on the cheek and back away so she can come out and grab her son.

I watch the two of them for a second before walking up the stairs towards my own space. The space is so much different than what I'm accustomed to. I'd get used to it, though. I'd do whatever I had to do so no one would ever find out about my past life. That woman is gone. Now, I'm just Sugar.

1

Sugar

"This is bullshit! Where is the rest of the supplies?" Bee curses as she leans over and shuffles through the boxes with the equipment that the little Furies would need to play.

"Are you saying that motherfucker cheated us? Raas! I'll kick his ass!" Riot jumps from where she's sitting and is on her way to the door when I catch her.

"Come on, babe, maybe it's a mistake. Why don't we call first and find out? He couldn't have done it on purpose." I soothe her.

"Bullshit, he did it on purpose. The man has a problem with everything that we're doing." Riot sucks her teeth and goes back to unpack some more equipment.

Eve's fury is more than just an all-female MC who doesn't

mind getting our hands dirty when the time comes. We also are advocates for people in our community.

Word is starting to spread. So much so we even have people reaching out to us to help with things we usually wouldn't be a part of. Recently, Melissa, a tiny teenager from town, trekked her way through the woods to talk to Vexx.

There's a community football tournament Melissa and her team of all-female players want to take part in. Since they're all girls, no one wanted to help sponsor them. They'd be the only girls in the tournament. I don't think I've ever seen Vexx say yes to something so fast in the time that I've known her.

Fighting for the underdog is what Vexx loves to do, and the fact that it's an all-girl team, she's all for it. What we didn't know is that being a sponsor to a football team is about a lot more than showing up at the game or letting the team wear your name on their jersey. We paid for the uniforms and equipment. We put the money down for the fees. Also, not to mention everyone else who didn't think an all-girl team should be allowed to play gave us shit loads of pushback. Of course, we still agreed to help, but it's more time-consuming than we thought.

"Bee, Mr. Bruce called. He said you left a box." Free calls from the kitchen where the phone is.

I chuckle and look over to the woman who was so upset, thinking we got cheated. "See, it's all good."

"Girl, I don't know how you always see the good in people. He better be glad he has the equipment though, I was going to TeePee the shit out of his store if he ripped us off." Bee jokes, and I laugh along with her.

"The game is tomorrow, right?" Addison asks as she checks off the equipment against the rooster that we have for the girls.

"Yeah, you thinking of bringing Glenn out with you?"

"Probably, if it's going to be a nice day. I need to get out of the house. All I do is sleep and feed him. The days are melting into each other at this point." She sighs and rolls her neck.

"For sure, and we'll all be there, so if you need any help with Glenn, you know that we'll be there to help." I smile at her and pat her knee as I continue to pull out the rest of the equipment.

"Sugar, you want to come with me to get the last box?" Press asks as he slips on his coat, "If Bee shows up, he may light the shit on fire."

I turn my head to look at her, "What did you do?" I squint at her.

"Nothing. I didn't do anything. It's not my fault he gets squeamish at the sight of knives. Especially ones stabbed into his counter." She shrugs her shoulder, and My mouth drops open in surprise.

"What the hell did you do that for?"

"Oh, come on, he was saying that everything wouldn't be ready until tomorrow. I knew he was bullshitting. I had to get him to move his ass."

"Baby cakes, you know there are better ways to get what you want, right?"

"Yeah, but this way is faster."

I laugh with her, but on the inside, I wish I could be as free as she is.

"Come on then, let's get this box before it gets too late." I grab hold of my wallet and follow Press out the door. "I know Vexx is going to want to have church later on when she comes back."

"Woman, bye." He calls up the stairs, and I hear Duchess slam the door in return.

"You make her mad again?" I ask. Press isn't the nicest person in the world, but Duchess is his pair.

"When do I *not* make her mad? I mean, do you know her? Breathing makes her mad." Press scoffs.

I hear Duchess's door open again, and footsteps come running down the stairs.

"Press." She calls out for him.

Duchess comes barreling towards us, and I have to move to the side, so she doesn't run me over.

"What the fuck." Press drops what he has in his hand in time to catch Duchess as she jumps in the air and latches onto him.

"Eww, you two, get a room," Isabelle complains from where she is sitting in the main area.

I hear Press growl out once before I throw my hands up and walk away from the area. "I have to agree with our little sister here, Duchess, get a little privacy if you're going to be loving on each other?"

"Stop being a dick." I hear her tell Press as she drops down from around his waist.

"Stop making me be a dick." He retorts. He leans forward

and presses a kiss to her mouth, "I'm sorry." I don't hear the last part clearly, but I can read his lips.

"Hurry back," Duchess calls over her shoulder before she bounds back up the stairs to her room.

"Now, are we ready to go?" I look to Press, who is still looking up the stairs in the direction his woman ran to. The love that neither one of them will admit to is clear on his face. I wish I had someone to look at me like that.

"Yeah, come on. Let's get out of here." Press shakes his head, and I follow him out of the clubhouse.

I get rid of the thoughts of me finding love. I didn't need it. I have more than enough love for myself and everyone else around me. All I needed was to stay safe and hidden.

Sugar

"Go, Melissa! Go!" Riot screams out. The crowd jumps up and down as Melissa runs with the ball for about half the length of the field. I'm not familiar with football, but everyone is very excited about what she just accomplished.

"I knew they were good, but fuck, I didn't know they were this good. This shit is crazy." Treble says out loud. Apparently, this is the going consensus to everyone in the stands. The girls were supposed to get knocked out in the first round. So far, they've beat every single team they've gone up against, and not by a little, they're blowing them out.

Proving once again that women can do anything men can.

After three games, the Furies are the ones to beat for the championship. They won the final match, Thirty-eight to three.

"Holy shit! That was awesome!" Bee grabs hold of Melissa and pulls her in for a hug when the team starts to make their way off-field.

"Thanks! It's all because of you guys!" Melissa smiles and looks around at the group of us.

"Aww, no. You guys are the ones that kicked ass." Vexx replies and tries to brush off the compliment. Her lips are smiling, but I can see that something is going on with her. She spends so long trying to be strong that I don't think I've seen her be vulnerable, not for the longest time. I'm going to have to find out if she's okay when we get alone.

"Melissa, is this them?" A woman with a microphone walks up to the star player.

"Oh yeah! I hope it's okay. The local news station wants to run a piece on Eve's Fury because you were the only ones that sponsored us. You guys deserve all the recognition in the world." Melissa looks over to Vexx for approval and begins to wave a group of people over to where we are.

My heart drops into my gut. The news? I don't want to be on the news. He'll find me. I start backing away, but Free grabs hold of my arm.

"Where are you going? Vexx wants us to get in the shot."

I shake my head and pull away again. I can't be in front of the camera. I never want to be in front of the camera again. "No, honey, I'll just sit this one out. No one wants to see me like this." I scrunch my nose and again try to pull away.

"Sugar, how can you say something like that. You're as beautiful as any one of us and you're family. Would you let me sit out because I thought I wasn't pretty enough?" Free pushes a strand of my jet-black hair behind my ear. "You're gorgeous and unique."

Unique, she's right about that. After I left Baxter, I did everything in my power to make sure that he'd never find me again. The tattoos, the piercings, even shaved my head so I'd look different. The crazy part is once I started changing myself, I realized that I was more comfortable being the wild one than conforming to what he wanted me to look like. I'd inadvertently stripped away all the false layers of myself, and now I'm able to let the real me shine through.

I'm proud of how I look, half a shaved head and all.

"Okay, I just didn't want to ruin the photo, that's all." I follow her back to the crowd where every one of the patched members and even Addison, who is only a prospect right now, is waiting for me.

"Come on, Sugar, your spot is right here." Riot indicated that I should stand right in front of her, and I follow her direction. Bright lights shine on us. The rest of the people from the stands clear out of the way. The reporter gets a few things ready with her cameraman, and then she goes live talking with Melissa and Vexx. They want to show how women can band together and do great things. Usually, I'm all for it, but right now, all I can think about is how I hope no one recognizes me.

It's been days since the football tournament, but we are still getting calls and gifts from random people both in and out of town. One of the local clubs even offered us a yearly pass for their VIP section. The owner said women as gorgeous and badass as us shouldn't have to wait to get into his club. I honestly think he was trying to get into Riot's pants, but we weren't going to turn down free passes to a club. Not the way we like to party.

"Let's do so more shots!" Bee stands up on the table and starts to dance to the tantric music playing through the speakers.

"No, you don't need any more liquor. We just got here, and you're already sloshed out of your mind." Free tries to pull her down, but Bee yanks her arm away.

"What the fuck are you, my mother? I'm not sloshed. I'm having a good time." Bee rolls her eyes and continues dancing.

"Why the fuck does having a good time include you showing everyone your ass?" Free hisses at her sister.

No one would ever deny that the two loved one another, but these sisters hated each other almost as much.

"Showing my ass? You fucking bitch-" Bee jumps down from the table and stands right in front of Free, ready to fight.

"Now, baby, we're not going to do any of that. " I grab hold of her and pull her with me to the bar. She could use water to cool off a bit. "Bee, you know your sister is only looking out for you," I say into her ear so she can hear me over the music.

"I can take care of myself, Sugar. I don't need her clocking everything I do. Doesn't she have her own little family to worry about? Where the hell is Jag anyway?" Bee crosses her arms over her chest and sits down on the stool I lead her to.

I wrap my arms around her neck and pull her close to me, "Bee, baby, you know that no matter what happens, no one, not even Jag, will be able to take your place in Free's heart. You're always going to be her number one. No matter what." I bump my nose with her and feel the tension in her body ease up a bit.

She raises her mouth and kisses me tenderly on the mouth. I accept the affection but know there is nothing behind it.

"I swear if you had the tools, I'd be all over you." Bee backs up and leans against the bar.

"I know it, sweets." I squeeze her thigh and raise my hand to get the attention of the barmaid.

I've already had this conversation with both her and Riot. Both of them like to have fun with me occasionally, but neither of them want to have a full relationship with me. It doesn't bother me. I love, love. Women, men, trans, whatever, it doesn't matter to me. I just want to feel loved and make sure that the person I'm with is loved in return.

I've never been the type of person that feels like love should be only what everyone expects it to be.

The bartender walks over to us, and I order Bee water and one for myself.

We sit there and sway with the music, letting the vibe of the place roll through us. We usually go to clubs a little closer to the compound, but based on the way Riot and Addison are on the dance floor sweating up a storm, we may need to come back to this one more often.

I turn to face the crowd, and the hair on my neck stands up. I let my eyes roam over the crowd of dancing people, but I don't see anything out of the ordinary. It feels like someone is watching me. I shudder and turn back to the bar, but I can't shake the feeling. With all the modifications I've made to myself physically, I'm used to people staring at me from time to time. This doesn't feel like that. Whatever it is, it's creeping me out. I turn again to look over my shoulder. I don't see anything that's not supposed to be there. I must be a little on edge because we're in a new place. My sisters are here, and everyone is having a good time. I have nothing to worry about.

I shake the feeling out of my mind and grab Bee's hand once she's finished drinking her water. We join Riot and Addison, and I dance all my worries away.

I have nothing to be afraid of, not when my family is here to have my back.

3

Sugar

"This is fucking bullshit, Roth! I don't have to fucking deal with this shit!"

Everyone besides Vexx and Roth is downstairs, and none of us know what to make of what's going on with the two of them. I've never heard them argue like this. I've never seen Vexx cry like this.

For the past few weeks, we've seen less and less of Roth. The odd couple that is our president and our one-time enemy are usually all over each other, but recently, something has changed. Roth would show up for a few hours and then leave again.

They never made their relationship official, but we all know how much they love each other. To hear them yelling at each other like this is strange.

Roth stomps down the stairs and gives each one of us a glance. His eyes land on mine, and though I want to be angry about whatever he's done, it's the first time I'm really looking at him in a while.

Roth is tired.

He's run himself into the ground trying to help Wire. He's trying to help the Wings of Diablo clubs. Trying to find any trace of the evil he was once a part of. The man is tired, and it's showing. I wonder if that's what he and Vexx are arguing about.

Roth nods once and walks out of the clubhouse. Jag moves from behind Free and follows him out.

"What the fuck happened?" Free asks before she darts up the stairs toward Vexx's room. Everyone else follows suit. I look out the window for a second and see Jag with his arms around Roth. Roth is leaning into the embrace. His shoulders are shaking.

That's not the stance of a man who wants to leave. It's the stance of a man who has no choice. I wonder if Jag will tell me what's going on with him. I doubt it, though.

I jog up the stairs and find the entire crew in the bedroom with Vexx. She's in the middle of her bed, crying her eyes out while Riot and Addison sit next to her, trying to soothe her.

My insides clench at the sight of our fearless leader breaking apart. She's curled into the fetal position and she's crying like her soul is being ripped from her body.

Addison looks up at me, her face covered in tears. I put my hand down and help her up. She's in no condition to help Vexx right now.

I hear the roar of a bike engine come to life, and Vexx starts to cry harder. Roth is gone.

I take Addison's place and pull Vexx into my lap, and finger comb her hair.

I rock her the same way I would a baby, not saying a word. I let my calmness settle her. I continue to rock with her until the room begins to empty. When the sun starts to shine through her window, and she's cried herself out, she raises her face to look at me.

"Sugar, you didn't have to stay in here with me. "

"Yes, I did, baby." I smile and scratch her head. "You want to tell me what's going on?"

"I don't know, Sugar. He's been pulling away for a while. I told him I noticed, and he said we couldn't be together. He never gave me an explanation. He just said that we had to stop. I don't understand. What is wrong with me? What is it about me that people find it so hard to love?" Vexx's eyes water again.

I grab hold of her face and kiss her cheeks, "Lana, that man loves you."

Her face crumbles in my grasp. "I thought so too, Sugar. I did, but if that's true why is he leaving?"

"I can't tell you why he's leaving, but part of me feels like he doesn't have a choice. He's leaving because he has to, not because he doesn't love you. Nothing will convince me that he doesn't. Something else is going on with him." I rub her hair, and she nods her head.

"I wish he would just let me in."

"Maybe this is the only way he knows how." I pull her

closer to me, "Whatever his reason, please don't think it's because you're not loveable. I've never met anyone who's more loveable than you, sweetheart." I continue to rock her, almost willing her to accept what I know to be true into her heart. I don't know what's going on with Roth, but I know Vexx's strong enough to pull through. I'm more worried about Roth getting through whatever is going on with him without her. I think he may need us more now than ever.

* * *

BY FOUR IN THE AFTERNOON, Vexx is more herself than she was earlier. Everyone is doing their best not to crowd her too much, but we are all on edge after what happened.

Vexx walks over to the small island and picks up her phone. It's been vibrating for a while now. "Shit," she pushes a hand through her hair and starts rushing to put on her boots.

"What's the matter?" I ask, pulling a bottle of water out of the fridge.

"Nothing. I got it." She replies too quickly. She hops, trying to get her foot into her shoe, and falls into the wall, unable to stay balanced. "God damn it!" She curses and lets her foot fall to the ground. She's trying to keep her calm, but it's clearly not working.

"Vexx, you need to relax. What's going on?" I take a step forward and smile at her. I don't want her to think I'm judging her. She's had a rough day. We all deserve a breather.

"I was supposed to do a pick-up an hour ago. Nick's been

blowing up my phone for the past hour. I didn't see it until now."

"I'll go." I'm already dressed and know where the pick-up is. I just didn't realize that it was today.

"No, I can do it." Vexx straightens up.

"I never said that you couldn't. I know you can, but so can I. We're a team here, Vexx."

She leans against the wall and gives me a stiff smile. "Thanks, Sugar. Do you want one of the girls to come with you?"

"No, let them relax." I'd only be picking up some medication for Tori, nothing anyone would put up a big fuss over. "I'll be there and back before you know it." I walk over to her, pull her into a hug, and kiss her cheek.

She squeezes my arm in appreciation. I make my way out of the clubhouse. When I get outside, I see Riot and Free going at it in our fight pit. It's been a while since any of us had to fight out our agitation. I'm glad to see they're making use of it. It's always better that they get it out instead of letting it fester amongst themselves.

Jag turns in my direction when he sees me getting on my bike, "You need back up?"

"No, I'm okay. Take care of them." I smile at him, and he quickly turns back around to make sure his woman doesn't get hurt. Jag lets Free do whatever she needs, but I don't think there has ever been a time when he wasn't right there by her side. The bond those two share is amazing.

I jam my lid on, and the prickly feeling I get when someone is watching me washes over me again. I turn all the way around, but I don't see anyone. Maybe it's a fucking animal or something. I don't know why I feel like this, but it's getting annoying as fuck. I start my bike up and ride down the hill.

I need to get this medication for Vexx before it gets too late at night.

Making sure I take care of this for her is more important than getting wigged out by some mysterious feeling.

4

Sugar

"Is this all of it?" I ask Nick.

Nick has been moving medications for us when Tori can't get over the Canadian border. He runs a supply store, so he has reasons to go back and forth from here to Canada.

"Yeah, it wasn't much this time." He picks up a box of shirts and opens it up, readying it for the shelves. I grab the small package and place it in my duffle bag. It looks like some b12 shots. It's the simplest shit that is the most expensive for Tori.

"Okay, thanks, baby. Let us know when we need to pick up the next shipment."

Nick nods his head and continues his work. I hear the small bell over the door ring to let him know that a customer has walked in, and again, that same feeling of someone watching me comes over me.

"What the hell." I turn in the direction of the door. I don't see anything out of the ordinary.

"Sugar, you need anything else?" Nick asks me as he walks over to the two women browsing the aisles.

"No." I look around one last time, "I'll see you later." I jog out the door and hop on my bike, ready to get back to the clubhouse. I need a drink or something.

I take the back roads to the clubhouse, because they're secluded and the scenic route always does a great job of helping me clear my mind.

It's only a twenty-five-minute drive back home. I focus on the road and the wind hitting my face. I'm too focused on what's going on ahead of me to realize that I should have been looking back. A loud revving engine is the only warning I have that someone is on my ass.

"What the hell!" I try to swerve and get out the way, but the car behind me stays on my tail. I speed up, trying to get away from the crazy driver. They stay right with me. I reach to my side for my weapon, but of course, I don't have it. I rarely walk around armed unless I have to be. I focus on riding hard, trying to move out of danger, but the car behind me keeps up no matter how fast I go.

I try to look through the window, but the dark tinted glass makes it so I don't see anything.

"What the fuck! Leave me alone!" I scream at the car as my back tire barely misses the bumper of the car behind me.

I look to the side and can see the steep ditch that I'm about to pass. It's a dangerous part of the road to be driving on, even more so when a crazy bastard is driving like a maniac.

I pat my pockets looking for my phone. I don't know if this is a threat against the club or just me, but I know I need backup. I pull my phone out of my pocket, keeping one hand on the handlebars. The bastard bumps the side of my bike, causing me to throw the phone and fight to keep the motorcycle level.

I try to keep my calm, but fear wraps around my throat. I don't have any other moves besides trying to get home as fast as I can. The car pulls up from behind me, and just as I think they are going to drive off, the vehicle swerves wide to the left before he swerves hard to the right knocking me clear off the road. I watch from my aerial position as my bike rolls down the hill. I say a little prayer as my body comes down hard on the unforgiving rocky surface. Rocks and twigs dig into my skin as my body tumbles much further than my bike. I can't hear anything but the wind whipping past my ears. I reach out, trying to stop myself from rolling, but the force of the hit is so great that nothing I'm doing is even slowing me down.

Pain shoots through my body as a sudden and loud crack of my back against a trunk jolts me to an instant stop. I try to inhale, but it feels like every cell in my body is crying out in pain. No air comes in or out of my mouth as I lay there in the dark, folded awkwardly against a tree that would not break. I hear footsteps and try to move, but the pain is too great.

The sound of my attacker gets closer, and I know that I need to get away, but there's no way. I close my eyes and let the darkness rush over me.

5

Sugar

My head hits something hard, and my eyes open slightly.

I'm moving, and whatever road we're on is bumpy as hell. I look around, and thankfully I'm not in the trunk or some shit like that. From what I can see, without moving around too much, I'm in the front passenger seat.

Another bump, and I hear someone curse sitting next to me. A voice I remember all too well.

Baxter.

I turn my head, and I can see his eyes straining to stay open. The bumping that I hear is the car going over a rumble strip.

I try to open the door. The second I touch the handle, something sharp cuts into my finger, and I hiss out in pain.

"What the hell are you doing, Diana! You're so fucking

stupid! You know how valuable those hands are?" Baxter reaches over and smacks the back of my head. The same way he always does.

"Don't you fucking put your hands on me!" I jump towards him and swing towards his face but have to hold back, one because my back is on fire and two because the man is driving a car with me in it. I want to get away from him, but I want to be alive as well.

Baxter grabs my hair and pulls my head back hard enough that tears spring to my eyes.

"You think I won't drive this fucking car off the road? I may not want you to hurt yourself, but I'll kill you myself before I let you get away from me." He glares down at me for a second, and even in that brief moment, I can see that he's serious. Baxter will kill me before I can get away from him.

"Test me, Diana!" He yells in my face, and I know better.

"Just calm down, Baxter."

"Don't tell me to calm down. I'm calm. Put your seatbelt on." He rubs my thigh, and I cringe on the inside. I hate that he thinks he can still touch me.

I reach over with my semi injured hand and pull the seat-belt on. I don't want to risk getting him angrier than he already is. I've seen him when he goes off the rails, and it's not something that I want to happen while we're in the car.

I don't feel anything in my pockets. He must have taken my wallet and keys away.

"What are you looking for, my love?"

"Nothing. I'm just a little uncomfortable." I do my best to take the focus off what I was doing. Just like he knows how to wind me up, I know how to get under his skin as well. Baxter has never been a man who just lets me need something. The problem is when he can't provide what I want, he becomes irate. It's so tough for him to realize that not everything I want he can provide.

He stuck in a deep breath, and I see him grip the steering wheel until his knuckles turn white. "What the hell did you think was going to happen riding that death trap on two wheels?" He says like he didn't run me off the road. I've only been in minor accidents on my bike.

"Don't worry about it, Baxter. I'll be fine." I give him a stiff smile and hope that it's enough to get him to drop it. I should have known better.

"Bullshit, you're fine. You're hurt." He sucks his teeth, and I can see his jaw clenching as he continues to talk through his teeth. "Now I have to take you someplace and get you better. It'll be more time away from the tour. We all know how much practice you need."

There's no use arguing with him when he's like this. I turn my head towards the window and hope that he's not too far gone already. I fell for Baxter because he believed in me, but I didn't realize his belief in me would push him over the edge.

Driving for about another hour, I'm happy to see Baxter pull into a hotel. Every minute he's on the road, I was sure he would drive off. He's tired. I'm not sure how long he has been telling me, but from the look of his car, he has been following me around for quite some time. I wonder how long he would have waited for the right moment.

"We're going to go into the reception office, and we're

going to get a room. If you try to signal the man behind the desk or make a scene in any way, I will kill them and you. No one will ever see you again." Baxter pulls me into a loving embrace, brushes the hair away from my face, places a chase kiss on my lips. "Do you understand, my love?"

"Yes, Baxter. I understand completely. I'll be good. You don't have to hurt anybody." He put his hand out, and I instantly wrap my hand in his. I've played this show with him millions of times before. No one would ever suspect that behind closed doors, this man is horrible to me. That's just how he likes it. We have to be perfect for the public eye.

Baxter always stays one step ahead of me, keeping me tucked closely to his side. We open the door, and the kind receptionist looks us both over before he asks if he can help us. I feel Baxter's grip tightened for a second before he replies. "Yes, we need a room for the night. I thought I would have enough energy to drive through, but the little woman here seems to think I need a bit of rest."

The man smiles and starts typing on his computer. I assume to find out if there are any rooms available for us. "Well, if someone as badass as her feels like you need a rest, I'd listen." He chuckles, and usually, I would laugh right along with him. I can't bring myself to because I know his one sentence is about to make my night a living hell.

"Yeah, she is pretty badass, right." Baxter chuckles along with the man and begins talking about the different types of travelers that come through here.

After a few minutes, the receptionist gives Baxter a room

key, telling him that this is the best room available. Baxter is the picture of perfect manners he always is.

"You two have a wonderful evening," the receptionist winks at Baxter, and my people-pleasing ex reaches over and shakes his hand like they are the best of friends. Baxter grips my hand as if he would like to rip it off the second we leave the desk.

"Oh my god, I wish I was brave enough to wear my hair like that." A woman says behind me as we wait for the elevator. Any other day I would have turned around and told her that she could pull it off if she wanted to. I'm all for female empowerment, but right now, I wish no one could see me.

I snap my jaw shut, just to keep myself from telling them to shut the hell up. Now instead of feeling proud of how I look, I feel judged.

I suck in a deep breath. Baxter is pinching my hand to get me to react how he wants.

I must not be smiling, or they must've said something that warranted a response.

I'm doing something wrong.

I turn around and shoot the girl a smile. She gives me one right back as she steps forward, clearly interested in my piercings and hairstyle. "Were you scared when you did that? I mean, did you think it would look bad?"

I answer truthfully, "Yes, I was petrified, but it turned out to be for the best." I was scared when I first decided to shave part of my hair, not because of how it would look but because it was my first real step in getting away from Baxter. When I'm with him, I always have to act a certain way. I have to dress a certain way. I have to say the right things at all times. Baxter is the epitome of control, and me cutting my hair was just one more way of me taking back some of that control. Now that I've found myself back in his grasp, I can feel that control slipping through my fingers.

"My love, the elevators here. I know how tired you are." Baxter stops pinching my hand for a second before he caresses my face lovingly and tugs me into the elevator.

"Maria! We found the charger." The woman standing behind me waiting for the elevator gets called by one of her other friends. She turns away from us and walks away. I exhale in relief.

The second the elevator doors close, I move as far into the corner as I can. Baxter doesn't follow me. He stays where he is. The elevators always have cameras. Over the years, Baxter has learned where the best places are to get me in check. At least that's what he calls it.

"What the fuck did you do to your hair anyway?"

"I was just trying something different."

"Different?" He snarls. "That's not different. You look like a fucking clown. How can I take you to events looking like that? What sponsor is going to want to deal with you now?" He shoves his hands in his pockets, and the doors slide open.

There is no one in the hall of our floor, and I contemplate fighting him right there. I may be able to outrun him, but I'm not going to be able to overpower him.

If he feels like he'll lose, he'll do something drastic, including killing both himself and me to make sure that I don't get away.

I cross my arms and follow him.

"Is that how you're supposed to fucking walk? Do you have an attitude?" He looks at me from the corner of his eye.

I drop my arms and pull my shoulders back. According to Baxter, a woman should always have an open disposition. Soft. It's the man's job to be hard all the time.

I want to laugh when I think about that. If he met Vexx or Riot, Baxter would lose his shit.

We get to our hotel room, and he pulls a pair of cuffs out of his back pocket.

"Baxter, listen to me. You can't keep me locked up in here. People are going to come looking for me. You know it's true." I try to back away, but I end up falling on the bed.

"I'm not leaving you anywhere, my love. I'm going to be with you every step of the way." He grabs my arm hard but not hard enough that it'll bruise. He puts one of the cuffs on me before he takes the other side and puts the cuffs on himself.

"Go to sleep. When we wake up, we'll get you dressed right and back in the studio. I can't wait to hear you tickling those ivories again." He leans over and kisses the top of my head.

I bite the inside of my mouth to keep myself from crying out. I never want to touch another piano. I spent so long being Diana Elgin, the concert pianist, that no one ever saw the real me. Sugar is who I am, and I can't let him rip me apart again.

6

Celia

"After another two hundred miles, I think we should stop for the night." Judd shifts in his seat and stretches his neck from side to side.

"Alright, babe. I think that's a good idea. I could go for something to eat." I absent-mindedly rub my stomach, and he swings his eyes in my direction.

"You're hungry? Why the hell didn't you say anything to me?" He heaves out a deep breath and turns back to the road.

Crap. He's mad now. "I'm sorry."

"Stop apologizing for things that you need, Celia. I've already told you, you needing something isn't something you ever have to apologize for." His words are harsh, but after a second, he reaches over and squeezes my leg. "I want to be able to give you what you need. That's all."

"You do," I answer right away.

He laughs and relaxes slightly in his seat. "I don't think that's possible if I don't even know what it is you need but okay if you say so."

I bite on the inside of my mouth to keep from saying anything else. I don't know what else to say. Judd is a gift from heaven. I'd put all the money in the world on that.

I've been in many relationships where the man only thinks about himself, and honestly, I've grown to believe that maybe that's just the way it's supposed to be. It's hard to break out of that mindset when you've been there for so long.

"What are you thinking about?" He looks over to me for a second before he turns back to the road. I gaze at him, his gorgeous beard, dark eyes, freckles, and his pull-on-me thick hair, and all I can think about is how I want him to pull over and lay me over the back of the car and fuck the hell out of me.

"Nothing. It's so pretty out here." I smile and turn back to the window.

"Yeah, wait until we get up to the coast. I can't say for sure, you know, but I think it's going to be so much different than what you're used to."

My stomach growls loudly, and I try to hide it.

"You're not going to say anything?" Judd just looks out to the front of the car.

"Judd, I'm okay. Let's just do the two hundred miles like you say, and we can pull over to eat then." I shrug.

"You know it's going to take me hours to get two hundred

miles, right? If you're hungry, are you going to wait all that time before you eat?"

I look over to him, waiting for him to drop the real question. When he waits for my answer, I know that was the real question. "Yeah, I'm not going to make any problems with that. I should be thankful that you're even worried about when I want to eat at all."

Judd doesn't say anything for a while, but I can feel the tension as he gets off the highway, and we pull into this small hotel. There aren't many cars.

"Babe?" I call for him trying to figure out what he's doing. That wasn't two hundred miles. That was barely ten.

"Let's go in here, Cel." I can see that his face is tight.

My heart drops, "You're mad at me now."

"For Christ's sake, I'm not fucking mad at you, Celia." He barks, and I jump in surprise. Judd is a large man. He's built like a fucking Ox. He spent most of his life in lumber yards swinging axes. It's one of the reasons I'm so drawn to him. I thought he would be the one to break me out of the shell that I'm in, but it's more of the same with him. I feel so different on the inside than how I act, but I just can't shake these inhibitions.

I look down and fold my hands in my lap. He takes his seatbelt off and turns to me. Quickly. Quick enough that I jump back.

The rage that lights in his eyes is scary as fuck.

"Celia, I know you've had some fucked up relationships. I know you've been through it, but I'm going to tell you this shit one fucking time. I'll never in my life lay a fucking hand on you. I'm your husband, not some fuckboy trying to be a man in these streets." He closes his eyes and takes a few deep breaths. "Babe, I love you. I want this to work, but if you don't trust me. If you can't put all you have into me and know that I'm not going to hurt you, how are we going to make it together?"

"I trust you," I whisper.

"Do you, Celia? Do you really trust me because I want this to work." Judd puts his hand on my face, and now all I see in his eyes is the love and need for me.

"I do." I lean forward and place a soft kiss on his lips, and it's all he needs to get revved up. He pushes me further into my seat and kisses me deeply.

I hear people walking, and I push him away. "Judd." I smile and put my face down to keep from showing how red I am right now. I love when he touches on me, but I'm so concerned about what others will think if they see us.

He smiles and moves back from me. I'm sure he's been with women who are much more outgoing than I am, but he's as patient with me as ever. I wish I could just let go, but that's not how I was raised. It's not what I was taught. No matter how much I just want to do all the nasty things I see in my head, I don't think I'll ever have the strength to do it.

Judd

I get out of the car and walk over to Celia's side. I didn't mean to get so mad at her, but really, it's so hard to love someone who's worried about hurting your feelings all the time. I was raised in a small town. Sure, I've had my share of women, but I don't think I've ever met someone who's as wholesome and sweet as Celia. Our love has been a soft rolling tide. It's never been wild and crazy, but if I could live every one of my days knowing that I put a smile on her face, I'd do it. It's why I was so quick to marry her. Sometimes I think I might have moved too fast. Not that I don't love her because I do, I just don't know if she's really comfortable with me. There are certain things that she does that bother me so much. I know she only does it because of past trauma, but how can I get someone to trust me when she won't even tell me when she's hungry. My friends and family all told me it would be a process. As much as I want to believe that she's getting better with me, part of me thinks maybe she isn't ever going to let loose. I don't know if I can live with the fact that she'll always live with that kind of fear in her heart.

"What do you want to eat? I think there is a pizza shop not far from here, and a diner too." I point down the road at the large diner sign rotating in the air over a small building.

She shoves her hands into her back pockets. "Pizza's good. I mean, you can have a chance to get some sleep."

"Sure, we'll get them to deliver it." I entwine my fingers in hers, and we walk over to the reception area. She's quiet when we get to the room and order the pizza. We talk about domestic things. How much gas we're going to need. How she didn't think she would enjoy the long trip as much as she has. When we're all talked out, we lay on the bed and have sex until we orgasm, and she cuddles into me. I love her. When I look at her, my heart wants to burst out of my chest, but I can't help but worry that she's not happy.

7

Sugar

I spent the night cuffed to Baxter, not knowing what I could do to get in contact with the club. Depending on how tired Baxter was, he can be out like a light, or he can wake up at the drop of a pin.

I've been tugging on his arm as much as possible just to see if he'll wake. So far, the most he's done is mumble and roll. The phone is right there. If I can even reach out to Vexx, I know they'll be here in a hurry. I hate that I have to depend on them to make this shit right, but I can't risk anyone getting hurt.

I put my hand out and see the bruises already darkening up against my arm from the crash. I'm so happy I didn't break anything, but every inch of my body feels like it's been put through the wringer.

I pick up the phone only slightly, making sure the headset is away from the receiver. When I hear what sounds like the dial tone, I start pressing the number to the club.

My palms start to sweat as I hear the first few rings.

"What the fuck do you think you're doing?"

I jump, not realizing Baxter woke up while I waited for the call to go through.

"You fucking bitch! I take you away from these dirty whores, and this is how you repay me!" He roars at me before he reaches over to the phone and hangs up the phone. I have no idea if anyone picked up the phone, and even if they did, they wouldn't know it's me.

"Baxter, I'm sorry I didn't mean it. I just wanted to let them know..." I try to explain myself in a way that will get through to him, but I know nothing will. There's nothing I can say that will ever be enough of a reason to Baxter for me to leave him.

"Shut the hell up! I don't want to hear one mother fucking word! Shut up!" He screams at me and picks up the phone that I'd just been trying to use. He snatches the entire console from the wall and begins slamming it over and over into my stomach and legs. I put my hands up to stop him, but he just keeps on hitting me.

"Baxter, stop!" I cry out. "Please!"

He brings his arms back, and in reflex, I use my free arm to elbow him in the face. He stumbles back, pulling me along with him.

What the fuck am I doing? I'm not some weak little girl who can't defend myself.

I fall on top of him and use my legs to knee him in his gut, and use my free hand to punch him in the face. "You fucking bastard. I hate you!" I scream. Baxter is used to the soft Diana. He's used to the woman who would cower in the corner the second he raised his voice. That's not who he ran off the road. The woman he ran off the road is a bad bitch who can take care of herself.

"Give me the fucking key! Now!" I grab hold of his hair and slam his head against the floor hard enough to rattle his brain.

"Okay, fuck, Diana, Okay." He reaches around to his pocket. Instead of him pulling out the key, he pulls out a gun with a silencer and presses it to my face. "Now, let's try this shit again."

I let go of him and try to back away, but we're still cuffed together.

"Open your mouth, Diana."

I shake my head no. I don't know what he's going to do, but I know it has something to do with that gun.

"You think I'm playing around with you?" He moves the gun away from my head and shoots. The bullet sails through one of the thin walls and into the bathroom, where I hear it stop with a loud pop. There's no sound from the gun, though. He can pump me full of bullets right now and no one would hear a thing.

"You've been gone too long, My love. I think they might have brainwashed you. I saw you on the TV. You know that's how I figured out where you were. I've been looking all over the damn world for you, and I find you in some backwoods town linked up with the trash. They made you cut your beautiful hair. Put all this shit in your face. They've taken my woman away from me, and I'll fight to get you back. Now open your mouth like a good girl Diana."

Tears stroll down my cheeks, but in the back of my mind, I know that if he's talking about fighting to get me back, it means he's not going to kill me. Not yet, at least.

I open my mouth, and he slides the silencer into my mouth. I watch his fingers the best I can, and I see that he takes his hand away from the trigger.

Another scare tactic.

I keep still because even though this is a scare tactic, I don't want to agitate him, and he pulls the trigger. I need to keep my cool right now.

"Now, this is what's going to happen. We're going to get some of the stuff I have for you out of the car, and you're going to get dressed. You're going to make your hair look presentable, and you're going to take all this shit out of your face. I have a meeting with Eli to get some practice in for you, and then I'll set up a meeting with some of the orchestras back home to see if they have any space for you. I'm sure they'll all be thrilled to have you. The press is going to have a field day." He pulls the gun out of my mouth and helps me up from the floor. There is a bit of blood on his face, and his clothes are rumbled up. Other than that, it looks like my attack hasn't done anything but cause him a slight inconvenience.

"I haven't played for a long while," I tell him.

I don't want to get wherever he sets up for me to practice, and he is surprised. Once I left Baxter, I left the piano player along with him. I will say I missed it. Music has always been my first love, and there is nothing that would ever change that.

"That's a shame, but I didn't expect much different. I mean, how the hell did you end up with that riff-raff? What are they called? Eve's Fury? What does that even mean anyway?" He shakes his head and pulls me to the bathroom.

I don't have the patience to explain what my club means to me and to each one of the girls that are a part of it. I watch him and every move that he makes. When he pulls down a washcloth from the rack near the shower and wets it, I cringe, knowing what he's going to do.

"Sit."

"Baxter, I can do this on my own." I smile at him, and the calm look on his face turns to anger at the drop of a hat.

"Are you saying that I can't take care of you, Diana? Is that why you ran away? Am I not man enough to give you what you need?"

"No, that's not what I'm saying at all. I know you can. You've always given me exactly what I need. All the time." I smile again and watch him calm slightly.

"I don't know if I believe you anymore, Diana. You always tell me these things, but then stuff like this happens? I don't even know why we fight so much. We're perfect for each other." He leans over and kisses me.

I can feel the passion building inside of him, but all inside of me is only disgust. If I could get the hell out of these cuffs, I'd try to kill him myself. Bring his ass back to Vexx so she could add to her collection.

I kiss him back, but after a few seconds, I pull away. I just can't bear it anymore.

"You're right. We've got so much to do." He wet's the washcloth and starts to wipe the blood, sweat, and old makeup off my face. "I can't wait until you see what I picked up for you. I got all your favorite designers. You'll be back to your old self in no time."

I smile up at him and let out a steady breath. That's precisely what I'm worried about.

8

Celia

I'm not pleasing Judd.

He says I am and that he doesn't want anyone but me, but I heard him in the bathroom last night jerking off. He thought I'd fallen asleep last night after we made love, but I didn't. Instead, I watched him sit on the edge of the bed with his head in his hands and deep sadness on his shoulders. I can count on one hand the different positions that we've tried when it comes to lovemaking. It's not that I don't want to do more or that I think he doesn't want to do more, but there is a deep-rooted fear inside of me thinks if I go down that road, he'll see me as a slut or something like that. I would never want him to think of me that way or embarrass him by having anyone else think of me that way.

No. I'm perfectly fine with missionary my entire life.

I tip-toed over to the bathroom door and watched as my husband stroked his long dick hard and fast. Nothing like the way he handles me. He came so hard that I was sure he would think he woke me up, but instead of coming out to check on me, I watched him hang his head low and just wash himself up. He's ashamed.

I don't know how to fix this. I don't know what it is in me that I'm missing, but I know my hesitation is wearing on my husband.

"What time do you think we should get back on the road?" I ask him from where I'm sitting on the bed. I'd fixed it this morning even though he told me that I didn't have to. He said that's what the cleaning service is here for. I couldn't just leave our room a mess no matter who they paid to clean it up.

"We can get some breakfast if you want. The diner?" His eyes raise as he waits for my answer.

"Oh no, I'm still pretty full from all that pizza last night." I was lying. I am hungry, but the diner will be so much money. Until he starts his new job, we have to be easy about how much money we spend.

"Cel." His face drops, and he looks away from me.

We had a long conversation about this last night. When I deny that I need things, especially the basic ones, he feels as if I don't trust him to take care of me. He says it hurts him. I don't want to hurt him.

"Okay, you're right. Let's go to the diner."

He smiles bright, and I melt on the inside. I wish I could make sure that he smiled like that all the time.

"Great, I'm going to wash up a bit, and we can be on the way."

I nod at him and pull my legs up to my chest. I flick the television on and end up settling on the news. I don't like to watch because everyone seems only to want to hurt each other, but I see a story about a young girl from a few towns over that is offered a scholarship because of her performance at a local football tournament. They went on about how an all-female motorcycle club is the reason her team was even sponsored in the first place. A feeling of pride in my fellow woman overwhelms me. I like to see stories like this. It's not very often that I see women doing such empowering things. I wish I were strong enough to do something as brave as that.

I hear the water splashing in the shower, and I think about what Judd must look like under the spray of the shower. Sure, I've seen him naked many times, but something about going into the shower and having him push me up against the wall to take me. I want him to take me as hard as he jerked himself off in the bathroom.

I'm his wife. Why shouldn't I just walk in there and tell him what I want? He's always telling me that I should. He says he wants to know what I want.

I want that.

I want him to force these walls down.

I want to be brave too.

A loud splash of water brings me back to the present, and I stand up on unsteady legs. I can do this.

My stomach clenches in both need and nerves as I walk over to the bathroom.

I move so slow trying to make sure that I steady my breathing. The last thing I want is to faint, and have him worry about that.

"Oh no." I stop in my tracks as I hear the water shut off.

My chance is gone. The door opens right away, and I'm left standing in front of the door way, staring at a towel-clad Judd looking like the cat who just ate the canary.

"Everything okay?" Judd tilts his head to the side and gives me a strange look.

"Uh... yeah... I mean, I thought I heard something. It must have been you coming out of the shower. Sorry." I turn and hurry over to the bed, busying my hands with making sure all the covers are tucked correctly.

"Okay," Judd walks over to his clothes and quickly throws on some clothes. I rush to grab the rest of his clothes and fold them up.

"Celia, I can fold my clothes. You're not my maid, you know." He shakes his head.

"I know, Judd. I just like to do this." I shrug and continue what I'm doing. He nods his head and lets me do what I'm doing.

I can't believe how close I was to making a fool out of myself. I let my heart rate calm down while Judd gets the rest of his stuff together. I don't need to be manhandled. I know what people would think if I let that little fantasy slip. No, I'm determined to be a proper wife. If that means we stick with the four or five positions he's shown me, I'm thrilled with that. At least I know I will be. I'll be whatever I need to be to make sure that I keep a good man like Judd around. I've been around too many bad ones to let him go because I can't control myself.

9

Sugar

I look in the mirror one last time and stop myself from crying.

I don't know who this woman is.

My hair is parted down the center so I can comb over a section and cover the part of my scalp that is shaved. I have on light eyeshadow and eyeliner. My lips are glossy, and all my piercings are gone. I'm wearing a golden brown, long-sleeved shift dress that comes right below my knee and a pair of flats I would have thought were cute had I been in junior high school.

I feel like I've gone back in time. I stiffen my shoulders and walk out the bathroom door where Baxter is standing waiting for me.

"That's still too much makeup. I want you to look presentable, not like a fucking prostitute." He grabs the back of my head and uses his handkerchief to start wiping some of my eyeshadow away. "I guess that's as good as it'll get. I think we need to think about getting you some plastic surgery. You're starting age."

My mouth drops open, and though I know that I'll probably get beat for saying something, I can't *not* say anything. "Baxter, that's life. I'm going to get old one way or another. I don't want to get plastic surgery for something that's going to happen regardless."

"I know what's best for you, Diana. You have a much bigger chance of breaking out into higher levels of the music industry if people think you're younger. I know it's a horrible way to think, but that's just how people are nowadays. Don't worry. I'll make sure everything is taken care of." He pulls me into a loving hug, and my body goes stiff.

"Like you took care of everything before?" I whisper, and he growls before he pushes me off of him into the wall. I put my hands up, ready to fight, but he's already got me by the neck before I can do anything.

"Diana, you were in pain. Every month. I fixed it, didn't I? Why the hell are you so damn ungrateful! You should be on your knees thanking me for making your life easier. Now you never have to worry about another fucking mouth to feed. You'll never have to worry about losing that gorgeous shape of yours. We can tour and live the life we always wanted."

Fucking delusional.

I don't know how I didn't see it before.

Back when I thought everything Baxter was typical, I let him rule my life. I listened to everything he said because he assured me it was for the best, and he was only looking out for me. I've had horrible, hospital visit-worthy periods my entire life. After one bout of killer PMS caused me to cancel an overseas gig Baxter set me up with, he brought me to a foreign doctor who diagnosed me with endometriosis. At first, I was excited because I finally had a reason why I was always in so much pain. I thought that I would get some medication, but the doctor informed me that my case was so severe surgery was the only way to help me. I didn't want to do it at first, but Baxter convinced me that it was the right thing to do. Still, I had my reservations about it, so he moved on to tell me that I was ruining our lives. That my selfishness was the reason that we were stuck in the rut that we were in. I got so many beatings over the two weeks it took me to decide to have the surgery. Baxter took all his time to come up with statistics and got all the information he could to make me feel at ease. He told me that they would only cut the damaged tissue. He said I would get a partial hysterectomy, and everything would be fine. We were still in a foreign country when all this was going on. It was hard for me to understand everything, but Baxter said he understood and would take care of everything.

The doctor informed me that it was going to be a hysterectomy. Some psychiatrists came in, social workers, but every time I'd ask Baxter why they were saying hysterectomy instead of partial, he said it was just the language barrier. I didn't question it. I signed everything I was supposed to sign. I went along with everything. When I woke up, I no longer had a uterus, they left my ovaries in, but everything else was cleaned out.

I cried for months. No matter how hard Baxter beat me, the pain of losing the possibility of having children never lessened.

It's a hot button issue for Baxter, and I know it. "You're right. I believe you. We can look into the plastic surgery." I say weakly since his hand is still around my throat.

"There, see." He lets my neck go, and my feet fall to the ground. "Things are so much easier when we work together, My love."

"I know. I'm sorry."

"You've already been through so much. You must be starving. There's a little diner down the block that we can stop in. What do you think about that?"

"Sounds good."

Baxter leans in and kisses me, his cock gets hard against my thigh, and I have to stop myself from throwing up in his mouth.

"You know, I think we may need to push breakfast back a bit. It's been so long since I've had you. No one else will do for me."

I moan when he finishes his speech. Not because it feels good but because I know if I don't, he'll say I'm cold and be angry for the rest of the day. I need to find a way for him to let his guard down. I can only do that if he's not put out with me. That doesn't mean I'm going to fuck him through.

"Baxter, I haven't had anything to eat for hours. I'd hate to get to the practice and not be at my best." I wrap my arms around his neck, and he kissed me again lightly.

"You know I spoil you." He squeezes my thigh, and I nod.

Fucking delusional bastard.

* * *

WE STOP at the gas station, a small shopping mart, and finally at the diner. There are people everywhere, yet I can't say a word to any of them. None of them can see through Baxter's smile and easy-going personality. I swear I could wear a sign that says he's a woman beater, and everyone would ignore it.

This is why I felt so trapped before. This is why I ran the second I had the chance and never looked back. No one is going to help me but me. The only problem is I don't know if I can wait as long as I did before until I break free. It's so much harder to be a victim when you've been the one putting the assholes in the ground.

The diner is pretty large; it's set up with a whole wall of booths and a few free tables. Almost every table is full, and the waitresses are running around trying to ensure everyone has what they need.

I sit back, and Baxter drops his hand to my knee and pinches me hard. Instantly, I sit up straight and plaster a polite look on my face. I'm in public; I have to act accordingly.

"What can I get you two?"

"I think I'll have a club sandwich and a seltzer water,"

Baxter answers. He reaches over the small table and takes my hand. "What about you, my love?"

Fucking snake. "I'll have a grilled cheese with bacon."

"Oh Diana, do you think that's the best? Especially everything you were saying about your weight? Maybe a salad? I bet the Cobb salad is great here." He looks up at the waitress for her approval, and she gives it.

"Yeah, and if you want a little treat, we have low-fat milkshakes, not as good as the real stuff, but it'll do in a pinch."

"Sure, that sounds great. Thank you so much." I smile at her and hand over my menu. The waitress finishes with us and hurries away to put in our order.

"Honestly, Diana, I just don't know what you're thinking asking for grilled cheese. Especially after the plans we made for you to get plastic surgery? I mean, did you think that meant you could go crazy with your body? I don't want to have to pay for liposuction as well." Baxter looks around the diner to make sure no one is paying me any attention.

"I thought we agreed that we would think about it? I didn't know it was a done deal." I keep my voice quiet. I don't want to draw attention. "Besides, I don't think a grilled cheese sandwich is going to put on that much weight."

"What are you talking about, Diana. You agreed to it. You were happy about the idea."

When the fuck did that happen? I think back over the conversation we had in the bathroom, trying to figure out when I had agreed to the surgery or when I said I was happy about it.

I know I never did, but the way he is speaking makes me

feel like I'm going crazy. Like maybe I did, and I don't remember.

"We really need to get you focused on more important things. I hate what those women did to you."

My heart starts to pick up in speed. I don't want him talking bad about the girls. They've done nothing but help me from the very first day I started with them. They saved my life when I had nothing, and they didn't ask any questions about it. To let him sit here and make it seem like they are the ones that did me wrong instead of him makes me want to jump across the table and slam my fist against his face.

"Stop tapping." He spits out at me through clenched teeth.

I look down at my leg. I didn't realize that I was bouncing my leg. I guess it's one way to get rid of the bad energy. When my eyes jump back up, I see Baxter eyeing the paper the man at the table on the side of us is reading. Baxter always likes to stay up on current events.

The man turns his face and looks at Baxter, "Would you like to read it? I'm about to head out, and I've read it already." The man offers the newspaper, and ever the gentleman Baxter graciously accepts it.

"Thank you so much."

I give a slight smile myself, but nothing that would come off as flirting. Baxter opens the paper, and I'm not surprised that I don't see anything about me in any of the headlines. Why would anyone make a big fuss about a little biker girl gone missing? The only ones I know for sure that are acting up are Vexx and the girls.

I keep my hand folded on the table and wait patiently for

my food. I don't want to look around too much, and Baxter thinks I'm trying to get attention, but I know if I keep my eyes glued to the table, it'll just cause more problems. Baxter wants me to be happy that I'm with him, not moping around.

I look up, and I see a couple seated at a table maybe four spaces ahead of Baxter and me. Both of them seem like they are tense or nervous. Just from their body language, it almost makes me believe that they are on a blind date. I think better of that because, one who goes on a blind date in the middle of the day and two, they have on wedding rings. They're married. I only hope it's to each other.

The man is very tall with a deep tan that makes me think he spends a lot of time working outside. Maybe he's a farmer? His jeans are weathered, and he's wearing a plain blue henley shirt. I can't see much of his face since his back is toward me, but he does have a head full of dark brown hair. Something like you would see in a shampoo commercial. I'm almost a little jealous of how thick it looks.

The woman he's with, though, is even softer than I ever was. At least she looks it. Her hair is light brown, and she has it pulled back with an actual ribbon. She doesn't have a spec of makeup on that I can see, and all of her clothes, though they fit, make it seem like she's deliberately trying not to be sexy. She's hiding too. I know that look. I don't know what she's hiding from. I wonder if she's hiding from the man sitting next to her, but when I see him touching on her and the way she smiles at him, I second guess that.

Looks can be deceiving.

I wonder how many people right now are looking at

Baxter and I like we are the epitome of a happy relationship. Maybe he is who she wants to get away from, and she doesn't know-how. I know I'm in a shit heap of trouble myself, but I can't just sit by if someone needs help. I don't know what I could do besides acknowledging her presence at let her know that she's not alone. Sometimes that little bit is enough. I know right now I wish someone would see that I need help.

The man that she is with gets up and walks toward the back. I'm assuming to the restroom. Her eyes follow him, and the smile that's on her face never falters. I think she's happy. Just as I'm about to look away from her, she catches my gaze. Her eyes settle on mine, and the smile goes away. I watch her suck in her bottom lip and bite slightly.

My eyebrows jump to my hairline. I know that look. She's attracted to me. I move my eyes from her for a second to check on Baxter. He's still thoroughly engrossed in the paper.

I turn back to her, and I see her face is down, and there's a bright red color to her cheeks. She's embarrassed. I love that. Being open to love, it excites me when I see someone else realize what they want. Usually, I would be helping her come to grips with her attraction at a time like this, but I'm stuck in this fucked up situation with Baxter.

I keep my eyes on her, and she looks back up at me. Her face is getting redder by the second. She tilts her head slightly, and then her eyes open wider.

I don't know what she says because she is so far away, but I see the word fury come from her mouth. She knows me. She knows me, and she's about to make a scene.

She swings her leg out as if she will stand, and I feel the

blood drain from my face. I shake my head no and look down. I hope she understands.

I glance back up at her, and she's staring harder at me. She glances from me to Baxter before she glances at me again. She knows my look just as well as I know hers.

"Help?" She mouths to me, and even though I want to say yes, I know Baxter has a loaded weapon. There's no way that I would let him hurt anyone in here so that I can get away.

"Something the matter?" Baxter asks, and I snap my attention back to him.

"No, just worried that someone crashed into my bike or something like that. I didn't have a chance to move it off the road. It's dangerous."

"Ah, no. Don't worry about that. I made sure that no one would see your little mistake." He turns the page on his paper just as the waitress walks over to us and puts down our food. I say my thanks, and Baxter reaches over to take my hand to say grace.

As he does, I wonder what he means about no one ever seeing my mistake. Did he make it, so they thought I was dead? Are they picking up pieces of my bike thinking that I was just burned alive? They must be fucking distraught. I can't wait any longer; I need to get out of here.

I glance back to the mousy-looking girl at the table and her shoulders are almost up to her ears. She's so tense.

I nod my head once and put a finger to my mouth to signify that she should be quiet. I don't know what this woman can do to help me, but I know whatever it is, I'm going to be ready to move.

10

Celia

I can't believe the badass biker from the eve's fury motorcycle club caught me perving out over her. Honestly, when I first saw a glimpse of her, it was those grey eyes that I was attracted to, then the full lips and the long black hair. Finally, the way it seemed like she was looking right at me.

My mother called me a heathen the first and only time I told her that I thought women were attractive. Since then, I've never voiced my opinion to anyone else. My second boyfriend caught me looking at a woman's naked body once in a fitting room. He told me I was a whore and dragged me out of the department store by my hair. We were all from the same small town, so no one called the police. The next time I was in the shop, everyone made sure to leave the dressing room before I got in. It was like I was a pariah or something.

The story on the news touched my heart. I guess it'd be okay if I let her know how much of an inspiration she is to so many people. I turn to stand, but I see her face pale, almost as if she's about to be ill at any second. She must know that I'm on my way over to her. She doesn't want me near her. It was such a stupid Idea.

I want the floor to swallow me whole.

My eyes jump back to her as she suddenly tenses up and looks at the man she's with. I can almost see the breath she releases when he looks away.

She looks so different from how she looked like on the TV. She looks uncomfortable. She looks how I used to look. There's no way someone like her could be stuck in a situation against her will. Where are all her friends?

I glance around and don't see anyone that looks like they might be in a motorcycle club.

I keep her glance and mouth the word help. I expect her to say no right away, but instead, she looks around like she's scared. A second later, the man she's with says something, and she answers, making sure to keep polite eye contact with him. It's phony as hell.

Once the mangoes back to his paper, she looks back to me and nods her head once before she puts a finger up to her mouth.

She is in trouble, and she wants me to be quiet.

I don't know what I should do. Should I call the cops, or will that be too loud? Should I go over and say something to her? Should I tell the waitress? Who can I turn to for help?

In all the times I've been trapped in a corner with

someone who only wanted to hurt me, I wished that someone would take the time to help me. I'm not going to ignore her now, especially when I know she needs help.

Judd. He'll know what to do.

I look at the woman who is still sitting with the man and have now started to eat.

I put a finger up where she can see to let her know to wait a minute. I don't want her to think I'm ignoring her. I clamp my jaw down to keep myself from throwing up. I'm not used to doing things like this. I'm not confrontational in the least, and even thinking this might end with her boyfriend wanting to fight makes me want to run away myself.

I can't back away, though. This could be my way to prove that I'm brave.

Judd walks up and settles into his chair. "Babe, you ready to go? Or do you want another coffee?"

I don't want to tell Judd that the woman behind us is in trouble while we're sitting here. Judd is far more aggressive than I am. He'll go right on over to where she is and demand to know what's going on.

"Cel?" He reaches over for my hand, and I pull away. I have to do something, and I'm running out of time. "Celia, what's the matter?" He leans back in his chair and just stares at me with a bit of annoyance on his face.

"Judd, do you trust me?"

He narrows his eyes at me, "Of course I do. What's this about?"

"I need something, and right this second, it's not going to make any sense, but I have to do it. Will you let me?"

He blows out a hard breath and puts his hands on the table. "Yeah. Is it illegal?"

I bite my lip and look to the side, I can't tell him everything, but I want him to be as prepared as possible. I reach over to his hand and squeeze, "Not illegal, but there may be some mad people."

"You won't hurt yourself?" He tilts his head to the side.

"No," I answer right away. I know he's not going to let me go if he thinks I'll get hurt. We may still be getting to know each other in this marriage, but I know that much about him.

"Okay. Go on." He sits back and just waits. I don't know how to react. I've never had anyone let me take the lead like this.

"I need the car keys, and I need you to pay, so when I come back, we're ready to go. Okay?"

"Yeah, where are you going?" He reaches into his pocket and gives me the car keys. He takes his wallet out of his pocket and pulls out a few bills to pay the bill.

"Bathroom." I pick his hand up and kiss his knuckles. It's the most public display of affection I've willingly given in my life. It's not that I don't want people to know we're together I just have never felt overly comfortable doing it. Right now, though, I don't care what anyone thinks but him and the woman behind him. "Be cool, alright." His muscles are tense, but he never takes his eyes off mine.

I slide from my seat and walk in the direction of the biker girl. I don't want to get too close to her man, but I have to get her away from him. Her eyes dart up to mine for a second before she looks back down at her food. I don't miss the fact that she's pressing her lips together so tightly not even the pink gloss she's wearing is enough to disguise the pale color they are becoming.

I clench my fist together and get ready to do the bravest thing I've ever done in my life. I walk by them, and at the last second, I turn my hip so I bump her milkshake. Just as I hoped, it falls all over her.

She jumps back in the booth, and the man she's with quickly reaches for some napkins to wipe up the mess.

"Oh god! I'm so sorry. So sorry. I'm such a Klutz. Let me pay for the dry cleaning." I tell her picking up some napkins and dabbing at the mess on her dress. She let's me help her but stares at me with those gorgeous eyes until she catches on what I'm trying to do.

"No, no, it was an accident." The woman says. "Nothing a little club soda and water won't get out." Within a second, a waitress has come over with the club soda and a rag. When I look back, I see Judd standing at our table, completely confused, but he doesn't make a move to come over.

"The bathroom is this way. Let's get you cleaned up." I turn stiffly to the man in the booth with her, "Do you need some club soda too? Did I get you?"

"No, just her." His eyes stare daggers at her as she stands up, and a big glop of strawberry milkshake comes rolling off her dress. "Come back fast. I wouldn't want your food to get cold." He says, but the way it comes out it sounds like it has a different meaning. It's a threat. He's worried about her getting away from him. That means if we don't move fast, he's going to come in that bathroom whether I'm in there or not and take her out.

The two of us walk towards the back bathroom, and I'm grateful when we walk in, and there is no one else in here with us.

"Oh my god. Thank you so much. I'll try to run from here. I don't know how far I'll get, but..."The woman starts to say.

"No, look." I pull her into the biggest bathroom and stand on the toilet, bringing her up with me. There's a window right above it. I push it open, and her eyes follow what I'm doing. I press the fob on the keys, and the lights shine for a second on the car, letting me know that the doors are open. "Get in the trunk. If he tries to look in the car, he won't see you. My husband and I will get you somewhere safe, and then you can call your friends. You're from Eve's Fury, right? I thought I saw you on the TV?" I slam my mouth shut to stop myself from rambling. I'm so scared.

"You don't have to do all this."

"I do, I've been where you are, and I wished that someone would have done it for me." I grab hold of her hand, and a zing of electricity passes through me. I'm worried, but this is the most exciting thing I've ever done.

"Thank you, sweetheart. You have to be save, okay. Tell your husband he has a gun. Don't try to fight him. He'll shoot. Do you understand me?"

I nod my head. I knew this was going to be dangerous, but I didn't think it would be *this* difficult.

"Go on. I'll stall him as long as I can." I push her to the open window.

"What's your name?"

"Celia, you?"

She smiles brightly, "Sugar."

I push her slightly to the window and watch as she runs to my car and hops into the trunk.

I hear plates and people talking but no loud commotion. Still, I bet her husband is somewhere nearby waiting for her to come out.

Time for me to play my part, "Yeah, just keep dabbing it with the rag. It's almost out. Luckily, it wasn't a chocolate shake, right." I fake a laugh and stomp my feet hard to mimic me walking out before I touch the door handle. "Yeah, sure, I'll let him know that you'll be out in a minute. I'm so sorry again." I say louder so that he can hear me.

I pull the door open, and just like I suspected, Sugar's husband is standing at the end of the narrow hall with a supremely pissed-off look on his face.

"Oh, there you are. Yeah, she had to take her dress off to get to the stain, but it's almost dry. She'll be out in a second." I tell him, making sure to keep as much distance as possible without making it look too obvious. I smile once and walk by like what just happened is normal. To an outsiders eyes, it would be. I only hope it's enough to fool him.

I time my steps to make sure I'm not running to Judd, but the second he sees me, he gets up and tries to ask me what's going on.

"Not now. Car." I hand him the keys, and I curl my hand around his elbow. I need some of his strength right now. It feels like my heart is about to pound out of my chest.

"How is she? Did the club soda work?" The waitress asks as she comes over to pick up the tip that Judd left for her.

"Like a charm. She just needs to dry up a bit." I smile brightly and tug slightly on Judd's arm so he knows we need to start moving. "Thank you so much."

The second the fresh air hits my face, I want to run to the car and drive away as fast as we can, but that would draw attention.

"Celia, god damn it, tell me what's going on? Should we be running?" Judd hisses out from the side of me.

"No, we need to be cool," I say, but my voice is shaky. My adrenaline is going a million miles a minute.

He tugs my arm, and we slow down. "If you don't want to run, you need to take slower steps. We're speed walking right now."

"Okay." I follow his lead, happy to have him by my side.

The car is on the side of the building, but it feels like it is miles away. Finally, when we get to the car, and he opens the door, I quickly slide in. Judd walks over to his side, gets in his seat, and turns the car on.

"Celia," he barks at me.

"Go!" I snap right back. I know Sugar's husband is going to figure out she's missing at any second. I'm gripping the center console and the door with all my might. "Judd, please."

"Fucking hell." He puts the car in gear, and we slowly start driving away. Just as we turn out of the parking lot and pick up a little bit of speed, I see Sugar's husband running out into the street behind us, calling for someone named Diana.

We did it.

I did it.

I helped her get free. I did something so many others never did for me.

11

Judd

In the past year since I've been with Celia, she's never acted like this. At first, when she said she needed to do something, surprised me. Celia is predictable most of the time. Now I can see how agitated she is and how she's about to rip the fabric off the door of the car, I'm getting pissed off.

"Celia, I'm worried. You're panicked. Did something happen with that man back there? Do you know him?" I ask thinking back to what I saw in the diner. I didn't intervene because she told me to be cool, but if that bastard did something to her, I'll turn right around and punch my fist through his chest.

"No. Um... do you think anyone is following us?"

My eyes nearly pop out of my head. What the hell did she

get us into, "Following us? No. Should I be worried about someone following us?" I can hear the tension in my voice.

"Just make sure, okay. I promise to let you know what's happening in a few minutes. I'm sorry. I had to do it. You don't understand. I've been on the other side. I just had to do it." Celia's entire body shakes, and tears pop out from her eyes.

"Don't cry. Whatever it is, we'll handle it okay. Just don't cry." I reach over and squeeze her leg, trying to give her some comfort. Our start together might not have been the most conventional, but it doesn't change the fact I'll destroy everyone to keep her happy.

I look in the rearview mirror, but I don't see anyone following us.

That doesn't mean I won't take Celia's concerns to heart. If she feels like someone might follow us, I'm going to make damn sure they have a hard time. I speed up and take some dangerous turns, some that have Celia squealing and clinging on to me like she's on a roller coaster. Part of me wants to laugh, but apparently, this is a severe situation.

I pull to the back of a movie theater and stop the car.

"Now, Celia, enough is enough. What's all this cloak and dagger mystery crap?"

"I'm sorry, Okay." She looks up at me, and I see the fear in her eyes.

"Cel, please, I need you to stop with this sorry shit. You haven't done anything that I know of. I just want to get out of the dark here."

"Okay." She sits back in her seat, and then I watch her open her car door.

"Where are you going?" I open my door and follow her out.

"I had to do it, Judd." I follow her with my eyes as she walks to the trunk. She clicks the release on the trunk, and I think maybe she stole something from the diner, but I didn't think that there was anything there that she could have wanted.

"Celia..." My mouth drops open when I see a pair of feet hit the floor and someone tumbling out of my trunk.

The woman she had the interaction with at the diner leans over and throws up.

My eyes nearly bug out of my head when she stands up and wipes the specks of vomit from the side of his mouth. "Where did you learn how to drive?"

I almost fallout right there.

"What in the fuck is this? Celia, what's going on. I need some type of explanation because I'm confused as fuck right now."

"The man that she was with is bad. I couldn't just leave her."

I hear what she's saying, and as a man who's been around countless women who have been in dangerous situations. Celia's right that she couldn't leave her. I would have turned around and gone right back to get her if she even thought to do something like that.

"You think he'll follow you?" I ask her.

"Without a doubt, but listen, I don't want you two to be dragged down into my mess. You've done enough. I can get myself together from here." The woman tries to back away.

"Nah, sweetheart, that's not going to go down. Come on. Get in the car." I put my arm out and wave her forward. "If you try to rush off now, I'm going to feel like I have to chase you, and I don't think that's the best thing right now. Let's just get off the streets, and then you can do what you think you need to do. I'm not going to leave you out here on your own."

The woman walks over to Celia, "He always so bossy?"

My wife laughs and grabs the woman's hand. "Yeah. Get in the back. Sorry, we kept you in the trunk for so long."

"It's better than being cuffed to Baxter."

I don't know who the fuck this Baxter is, but just that one sentence is all I need to know that I will beat him down the second I see him.

Celia

Sugar jumps out of the trunk, and from the very second that she puts her hand in mine, I know that we're going to have a bond. I can feel her strength trying to push through her. I pull her into the car and get her settled into the back.

"Do any of you have a cell phone I can use? I need to call my club."

"Club?" Judd turns the car back on and looks over his shoulder at her.

"Yeah, this is one of the women I saw on the news. She's part of a motorcycle club. She looks a little different." I look over my shoulder and watch as Sugar finger combs her hair to the side to show the shaved part of her head. She's gorgeous.

So damn gorgeous.

"Take my phone; I'm going to find us a hotel to lie low in until we get you straight."

I reach into Judd's pocket, pull out his phone, and hand it over to Sugar. When the small electronic device falls into her hand, she doesn't move for a second. She just looks up at me with tears in her eyes.

"Thank you, Celia. The both of you."

I reach over and grab Judd's hand. I don't think I've ever been so proud of myself.

"Of course." I try not to let the excitement creep up into my voice, but I've never done anything like this.

"Absolutely," Judd replies as well. I look over at him, and something in his pants catches my eyes. He's hard.

For the briefest of seconds, I think maybe it's because of Sugar. I wouldn't blame him. She's beautiful, but when he's not looking at the road, the only person he's looking at is me. We're probably in the most dangerous situation either of us has ever been in right now, and I'm turning him on. Now I can't hide the smile on my face. Even with the breathtaking woman in the back, this man still only has eyes for me, and something about what I've done in the past few minutes has turned him on enough that he looks as if he might throw me on the side of the road and take me in ways I'll never be brave enough to ask for.

12

Sugar

Judd and Celia have literally saved my life. She doesn't know me from Eve, yet she put everything on the line and help me.

They've given me a phone to use, and I quickly punch in the number to the clubhouse.

"Yeah." Bee answers.

"Hey baby, is Vexx there?" I nearly cry when I hear her voice.

There's a long pause on the line before she speaks again, "Sugar?"

"Yeah, love. How are you guys doing?"

She huffs out a breath before she continues talking again. "Are you fucking kidding me? Do you think you can just do that and then call back like everything is all good?"

I pull the phone away and stare at the receiver like it's

going to grow another head. "What're you talking about, Bee?"

"You sent your new man with your patch and a note talking about you were never really a part of this family. How you were only here to fill a void, and now you know it wasn't up to us to do that. How sorry you are. All..."

The bullshit. I can't believe Baxter went through that. When did he do this shit? I know that I don't know where my patch is. Maybe when I was knocked out, he went back? I have no idea.

I cut off her spiel. I know how upset she is, especially if they were all on the assumption that I had abandoned them.

"Baby girl, it's bullshit." I raise my voice to get over hers.

"What?"

"All bullshit, orchestrated by my asshole ex. I'd never abandon my patch, and right now, I need some backup."

Another deep sigh comes through the line. This time attached to it is a relieved giggle. "Really, it wasn't you?"

"No, Baby. I'd never."

"Backup, wait, your ex came for you? Oh shit. Let me get the girls."

I hear a bunch of rustling and finally Bee calling for church through the house.

"What the fuck is going on?" Vexx's voice calls out, and I hear Bee telling them they need to just get to church. No one has ever left Eve's fury, so I don't know the protocol for someone who leaves the club. I'm sure talking to them on the phone is out.

I hear a door close on the other end. I look up to see Judd

and Celia giving each other the hottest looks. Part of me wonders if they do things like this on the regular. Either way, I'm eternally grateful.

"What the hell do you think you're doing calling church Bee? That's not your fucking place." I hear Vexx snarling. At least I know that Roth and her breaking up didn't stop her from being a hardass.

"Look, I know what everyone said, but just listen, okay, Sugar is on the phone."

"Nope! Get the fuck out of here with that shit."

"Are you kidding me?"

"She's got some fucking nerve!"

"Shut up!" That last order is from Vexx, "Everyone sit in your fucking seat and shut up. Bee, we discussed what bringing Sugar up would do. So either you have some new information for us, or you're going against a direct order."

"She didn't leave. Her ex orchestrated all this. She's in distress."

"Fuck, I knew it." I think Riot says.

"What the fuck do you mean you knew it!"

After that, I can't make anything else out. They are all arguing so much.

"Shut up! Is she still on the phone? What the fuck are we doing?" I hear more ruffling and then a button push.

"Hello?"

"Sugar?"

"Vexx, hey, baby."

"Did you write that pussy ass letter?" Her voice is stern.

"No. I'd never. I went to pick up the meds from Nick, and

my ex must have been stalking me because, on my way back, he ran me off the road. He tried to make it like things were going back to normal. I only got out because of two angelic Samaritans who let me hide in their trunk." I get out as much information as I can.

"Thank god, where are you?"

"I'm..." I look around, but nothing looks familiar. It's only then that I realize I don't know where Baxter has taken me. "I don't know. Hold on."

"Celia, where are we? What state is this?"

"Uh..." The woman looks over at her husband. They must not be from around here.

"We're in Vermont. We were on our way to Maine."

"Vermont!" I yell out in surprise. "Oh, boy." I lean my head back. I didn't realize Baxter drove all this way. That would explain why he was so tired when I woke up.

"Vermont? Jesus. Okay. We're in a bit of trouble here, but Bee, Riot, and I will haul ass up there."

My palms get sweaty, and I grip the phone tighter. "What do you mean?" What the hell is she talking about? They were in trouble up there? "What's happened?"

"Last night, the feds raided Tori's house. They found some of the medication. Luckily, it wasn't her entire stash, but they took Tori, Jag, and Press to lock up because they were there. Tori and her hot-ass temper went off on one of the officers, so they're holding them right now without bail. It seemed like a setup. I won't lie. Based on the letter that we thought you sent, it sounded like it was you who set us up.

"No, sweetheart, I'd never do anything like that." I shake

my head vehemently, as if she could see through the phone waves.

"I knew that, but I guess we just needed confirmation. Can you get to the cops? Do you want to do that?"

"Yeah, I can give it a shot." At least if I had to wait for the calvary to come, I could do so in the safety of the police station.

"Okay, last I heard, Wire and his nomads were on their way up to the Boys of Djinn MC in Maine. If worse comes to worst, you can go up to them. I'll call them so that they can keep an eye out."

"Got it." I sigh hard; this is what I'm used to—fixing problems. My family loving me. Things I thought I once had from Baxter. "How are you doing, Vexx?"

She laughs softly. "Girl, you the only one I know who's just been in a traumatic experience that's more worried about everyone else than yourself. I'm good, Sugar. I'll be better when you're back home. When all my family is back home."

"I know, I'm working on it. Tell the girls I love them and kiss Glenn for me."

"Will do. Make sure you keep in contact with me. That's a fucking order. I don't want to have to kick doors in trying to find your ass. Got it?"

"Yes. I'll contact you every step of the way."

"Love you, Sugar."

"I love you too, babe." I end the call and hand the phone over to Celia.

"You have a boyfriend or something there?" Celia asks when she takes the phone back.

"No, not at all. Why would you assume that?"

"Well, you seem very… I don't know, loving?" Celia turns in her chair and squints at me slightly.

"That's just me. I love everyone. Love is probably the easiest, most impactful gift you can give, and it doesn't cost any money. I think everyone should know love, no matter who they are. It's why they call me Sugar." I shrug.

"So, what's your real name?" Judd asks.

"Diana."

"Yeah, you seem so much more like a Sugar," Celia says before she turns back in her seat.

"Do we have a plan, are your friends coming to get you? What do you need us to do?" Judd asks.

"Let's get the hotel. I'd rather get off the street in case he is following us, and then tomorrow I'm going to the police to press charges." I put a hand on both of their shoulders and squeeze. Judd jumps slightly, but I soften my touch. "Thank you both for this. You didn't have to get involved."

"Of course we did. No one should be left alone to face something like that. I'm just happy we could help."

"Yeah, I can't fucking stand men like him. He should rot in prison." Judd clenches his jaw as he pulls onto the interstate.

I don't know either of these people, but I feel safer now than I have in days. I shouldn't. I thought Baxter had given up searching for me before, but now I know he's never going to stop.

13

Sugar

Judd managed to get us checked into a beautiful bed-and-breakfast. It was far enough away from the main traffic I felt good about Baxter not being able to find me.

I'm bigger than Celia in pretty much every way, but she has a pair of leggings and a shirt she says I can have. I have to hand wash my underwear and bra, but I'm okay with that. At least I was out of those awful clothes. I didn't have any of my earrings, but I can always pick those up later. Right now, all I want to do is get home.

I spend most of the night just observing Judd and Celia around each other. It's clear that Judd adores her, and Celia is the same for him, but something seems to behold both of them back from really expressing themselves. It almost feels like they are both in an interview, both trying not to overstep. It's the strangest thing I've ever seen.

"Babe, I'm going to run over to the supercenter I saw an exit back and pick up a few things. Do you want anything?"

"No," Celia answers right away.

Is she scared of him? Even though I see how they act around each other, sometimes it seems as if she thinks he's going to get mad or something like that.

"You sure? Don't you want any snacks or anything? There's not much around here."

"I'm fine, Judd. I don't want to cause any more trouble than I already have." She replies and smiles.

Oh, no. no-no-no. This won't do.

"Actually, do you know what eyeliner is?"

Judd scrunches up his nose like he just smelled something disgusting. "Those pencils girls use on their eyes."

I laugh, "Not just girls baby, I've seen Pete Wentz wear it better than some of the best models."

He chuckles and shrugs, "Yeah, I know what it is."

"Can you pick me up a black one? No matter the brand, the store usually has them for a few dollars. I'd really appreciate it, sweetie."

"No problem." He looks back over to Celia, probably waiting to see if she changed her mind. She says nothing.

Judd nods once before he turns to walk out the door, leaving Celia and me in the room alone.

"Do you need me to do anything for you? The owner said there was still a bit of lunch leftover that we can have. I can bring that up to you?" Celia rubs her hands down her thighs.

"No, baby, I don't need anything. Can you sit here and talk to me?" I sit on the bed and tap the space next to me to let her know where I want her. She complies immediately.

I don't say anything, just wait for her to come out of her shell. She's so quiet. I don't want to push, but I have a feeling she doesn't think very highly of herself.

"How long have you been with your Ex?" she asks but then quickly tries to take it back. "I'm sorry, that's so rude. It's none of my business."

"Celia, it's all of your business. I'm not going to hide anything from you." I rub her arm, trying to ease her mind. "I've only been with him recently for a few days. I'd run away from him about two years ago. That time I was with him for almost five years. He was my entire world, and I didn't even know it." I look off to the side and reminisce about the early times in Baxter and I's relationship. I didn't see the bright red flags then. I thought he loved me and that I loved him.

"I understand that." She nods, not even looking at me.

"Yeah, I sort of figured. As messed up as it is, I can almost point out a woman who's been hurt by someone they loved in the past. Something in the eyes." I raise my hand and caress her cheek quickly before I let my hand fall back down to my lap.

"Yeah, I've had three boyfriends in my life. Unfortunately, there hasn't been one that hasn't either beat me or told me how worthless I am. I guess I know how to pick them." She smirks.

My spine stiffens at the comment. "What about Judd? Is he one of them?"

"No, not once. Judd has done nothing but take care of me from the very first second we've met. I'm almost too lucky to have someone like him." A wistful smile replaces the slight smirk she was just wearing.

"How long have you two lovebirds been together?"

"Oh, about a year now. We had a speedy courtship."

I pull my knee up on the bed and turn towards her. "Lots of wild times?" I joke with her.

"No, not at all. I'm not a wild times kind of girl. We made a mistake the first night we made love. I wound up pregnant, and we were married two days later."

"Wow, That is quick." I look around, the obvious question in the air, but one I don't want to ask. "Where's the baby?"

She cringes, and her hands grip onto the bed. "We lost him. I miscarried at four months. It's been hard, but that's why we're on this trip. Judd thinks a new start in a new place might be just what we need."

I pull her into a deep hug, not even caring that she's stiff as a board. She's not used to love. I've got more than enough to give. "Baby girl, I'm so sorry. I know that'll never take away the pain, but I hope you know it wasn't your fault."

Finally, her shoulders slump, and she hugs me back. Her body realizes that I'm not a threat. "It feels like it sometimes." She admits.

I pull her away. "It's not. Don't break yourself down thinking about all the things you could have done differently."

She smiles and shuffles a little closer to me. "What about you? Do you have any children?"

"No, I'm not able to, but I hope one day to adopt. So many children are starving for love out in the world."

"Is that why your ex is so upset? Because you can't have children?"

I roll my eyes, "No, he's part of the reason I can't have children, but he's upset because he wanted me to be something that I don't want to be. He had my life planned out, and when I first met him, I thought it was what I wanted to until I realized who he thought I was and who I am are completely different. Baxter thought if he beat me enough, I'd get out of my rebellion. It almost worked too. Until I ran away and joined up with Eve's Fury."

She reaches over and grabs my hand. "Is that why he changed you into those clothes? You look so different from the picture on the news. It was those eyes that caused me to remember."

I tilt my head, "My eyes?"

"Yes, they're beautiful. I've never seen eyes as pretty as yours." Celia focuses on my mouth and slowly licks her lips. I knew I wasn't going crazy before. She is attracted to me. Unfortunately, there's nothing we can do about that, she's married, and her husband is one of the folks who saved me. I don't want to do anything that would be disrespectful to him.

"Thank you. Your eyes are beautiful as well."

She laughs and blushes hard. "Please. I'm as plain as they come. I don't know what Judd sees in me. He can have anyone he wants." Her mouth closes quickly, leading me to believe that she had more to say.

"Did you think he would leave after you guys lost the baby?"

Her eyes open wide. "Yes, I still do. There's nothing about me that can hold him."

"You don't need to hold him, baby. That man's stuck to you. He's not going anywhere. I can see it in the way he looks at you." I wink at her.

"You think so? I don't know. I don't think I'm enough for him. He's never complained, but I know he's not all the way happy. He treats me like a princess, but I see he gets frustrated sometimes. I don't know what I can do to be more like what he wants." She crosses her arms over her chest.

"Love, that's the problem right there. Has he told you he wants you to be something more?"

"No, of course not."

"Then why do you assume he does? I'm not psychic, so I don't know what he's thinking, but I will say it seems like the both of you are holding back. I think he truly loves you, and no matter what you do, he's not going to stop. You've got a good man there. Open up to him, let him know you love him. Let him feel how you feel." I grab her hand and press it to her heart.

"What if he doesn't like it? What if it pushes him away?"

All these fears. I know from experience that they come from past relationships, but if she doesn't want to spend the next decade or however long she takes to realize who she is on the inside, being scared, she needs to hear some hard truths.

"Sweetheart, if that man wanted to leave you, he would have done it already. Nothing is forcing him to stay. If he doesn't like it, he'll say. Though I don't think any form of affection is going to go unwanted." I laugh slightly and scratch the side of her leg.

"He's too soft with me."

My eyebrows jump to my hairline. I would think she likes soft, but wanting him to be a little rougher isn't something to be ashamed of.

"Do you tell him?" I ask, keeping anything that even resembles judgment off my face. She's opening up to me, so the last thing I want to do is make her feel like I'm judging her.

"No, never. I can't get the words out. Every time I try, I get choked up and start thinking about everything besides what we're doing."

"I understand. Well, there may be other ways to get the hint over to him. Would you ever think of taking control?"

Her eyes open wide. "What, like me on top?"

"Yes."

"No, I've never. My ex said it made me-"

I put a hand over her mouth to stop her from talking. "No, absolutely not. I want you to take every single negative thing that any of your exes have ever said to you and throw it away. All you need to think about is what you feel about yourself. If you want to try being on top, it doesn't make you any less of a woman, it doesn't make you a whore. It's just what you like; I'm sure Judd wants to be a part of the things you like. He wants to know what you want."

She nods, "He does, at least he always says he does." She flops back on the bed. "I wish I weren't so scared all the time. I wish I could be brave."

I lay down on the bed with her, putting a little space between us. "What makes you think you're not brave? From what I've seen, you're one of the bravest people I know."

"I'm not. I second guess everything I do. Heck, I can't even kiss Judd without wondering if it's enough for him. I want to walk in the room and not be afraid that everyone is judging me. I want Judd to feel how I feel inside when I think about him touching me. I want to experience things with him. I want to be...."

"Free," I say for her.

"Yes, I feel trapped in my mind, and it's nothing of his doing, but I don't know how to get out. He can tell, and he doesn't deserve half of me." Her breath is shaky towards the end of her confession.

I can't fix all her problems. She may need to see a therapist or something like that, but I can help her with other things.

"Why are you afraid to kiss him?"

"Oh, I don't kiss him right, at least I don't think so."

I turn on my side to her. "Why?"

"I don't know. I mean, I guess I feel too vulnerable. Things feel good, and I want more, but I don't want him to think I'm a-"

I cover her mouth for a second time. "If you call yourself a whore or anything like that again, I'm going to be very put out with you, babe. You're his woman. If there is anyone in this world that you should show how much they make you feel good, it's him. From what I know about the opposite sex, the good ones always want to take care of their partner. It makes them feel good. Don't you want to take care of him, see him completely blissed out?"

She nods and pulls her bottom lip into her mouth.

"I know you do. Just try things slowly and when you feel good, just tell him or show him. There is nothing wrong with you feeling good. Nothing to be ashamed of." I rub her upper arm, trying to keep my touches as platonic as possible, but all this talk about making people feel good and the way her cheeks turn that beautiful pink color is turning me on.

"What makes you feel good?" Her voice is soft.

I cross my legs and clench my thighs; I need to stop this. This is Judd's woman I'm not into home wrecking, no matter the gender of my partner. I won't act, but I can talk about it.

"I love hands on my body. I like to hug and kiss. I want to feel how much my partner wants me. I want to be consumed with my need to have them. I want passion. I crave it. Man or woman."

Now her eyebrows are the ones that jump up, "Both? You like both men and women?"

"I love all people. Another part of my rebellion that Baxter tried to beat out of me. He didn't like the fact that women turned me on."

"My mother told me it was a sin."

I grin, "Sorry to go against your mother, sweet cakes, but we're all sinners."

She smiles widely. "I've always thought it was wrong that I'd get turned on by a woman. I've never been with one before, but I want to experience it." She moves closer, and I have to lock my hands against my legs to keep from moving closer to her. She's so gorgeous, and our adrenaline is all over the place from everything I'm putting them through. I don't want to take advantage. I'm lying; I do want to take advantage of her. I want to take her any way she wants to give herself to me, but I won't.

"You will. Judd may even want to help you bring that fantasy to life."

She moans slightly. "You think so? No. He'd never."

I swear someone could knock me out with a feather right now. Who would have thought this skittish, self-conscious woman would be open to bringing another woman into her bedroom. I've always known it to be accurate, but Celia is just another example of how sometimes it's the quiet ones you need to watch out for.

"You'll never know unless you ask. As long as both of you communicate openly and are willing, I doubt there is very little he won't do for you." I say this to ease her mind, but Judd could be someone who isn't very open-minded or just doesn't like to share. It still holds that she won't know until she asks.

Heavy footsteps thud on the stairs that lead up to our room, and Celia jumps out of bed like we had our tongues in each other's pussy.

I want to laugh, but I don't want her to feel any more self-conscious.

Judd walks in the door, and his eyes instantly go to his woman. I see them flash with desire before that spark dies out and turns to adoration. I love to see love. He loves her, and he's hungry for her.

"Everything okay?" He asks as he looks away, puts the bag down in the chair, and locks the door behind him.

"Yes." Celia answers. She's stiff and barely looks at him.

He won't make a move, and neither will she. Lucky for both of them, I know all the moves to make.

14

Judd

The second I walk into the room, I know something is off. Celia is standing in the corner, and Sugar is lying on the bed. When I look at Celia, she can barely hold my gaze.

The crazy part is I don't know what could have happened in the time that I've gone to the store and come back that would cause Celia to act like this. It's so hard to read her. Every day, it's like I'm trying to decipher a puzzle, and I'm not getting any closer to figuring out the answer.

"You sure everything's okay. You seem tense." I walk over to Celia and put my hands on her arms.

"Yeah, we were just talking. I didn't expect you to come back so quickly."

Now I'm even more confused. Why should it matter they were talking? Maybe I'm missing something.

"Okay. Do you want me to leave? You two can have some girl time." I lean down, trying to look into her eyes. I know sometimes girls like to just chat with other females about things. Since we've been married, I don't think Celia has visited with one friend. She's a very lonely woman. It would be fantastic for her and Sugar to spend some time together.

"Uh, sure. If you think that's best." Celia looks up at me and gives me her typical gorgeous smile.

"Okay, I can go downstairs to the main area. There's a small library down there."

Sugar sits up on the bed and clears her throat slightly, a tight smile on her face, "Celia honey, is that really what you want?"

I turn my head back to Celia. Did she want something different? I hate this. I just want her to be open with me. I want her to tell me what's going on without me always having to guess.

Celia turns to Sugar, and her eyes open wider a bit.

"All you have to do is to be honest. Is that you want, Celia?" Sugar asks again.

Celia shakes her head no, only slightly.

Sugar stands and ambles in our direction. "Don't tell me. Tell him. Tell him what you want."

Celia looks at me, but almost instantly, her head drops until Sugar stands behind her and lifts her chin.

"Baby, I promise there is nothing you can say to this man that is going to make him turn away. Trust him." Sugar speaks directly in Celia's ear.

Celia tugs on the bottom of her shirt, "I want you to stay." Her voice is so low I can barely hear her.

"Okay, I'll stay." I take a step forward, but don't pull her toward me. She doesn't like people seeing us being affectionate. "That's what you 're so nervous to tell me?"

"Can I help you?" Sugar asks Celia, who nods immediately.

Help her? Help her with what? "What's going on?" I ask both of them?

"Celia just needs a little support, direction, if you will. No worries, sweetheart, she's running the show." Sugar replies, shooting me a wink.

Sugar reaches out and grabs my hand, pulling me closer to my wife. She raised my hand and put it on Celia's neck.

"Judd, do you want your wife?"

"Excuse me?" My first instinct is to get fucking offended. I barely know this woman. Who the hell is she to question how I feel about my wife.

Celia backs up slightly, her body tensing.

"No, baby, I *know* you do, but I want her to hear you say it." Sugar's voice is sensual, like an erotic song I want to dance to.

I look back to Celia, who is still looking at me. She is waiting to see what I do. "Yes, I want her. All the time." I admit, though, I didn't think it was a secret. Did Celia not know how badly I always want her.

"Do you want him, Celia?" I hear Sugar ask to which Celia nods.

"No, you don't get off that easy. Tell him."

Celia gulps and licks her lips before she talks, "I want you, Judd."

Sugar looks over to me, "Judd, maybe a kiss for your woman?"

I still don't know what's going on, but my body is loving it. I lean down and search Celia's eyes for approval. When she tilts her head up, I brush my lips against hers.

Celia wraps her arms lightly around my neck, and like usual, the second I try to deepen the kiss, she backs up. Except this time, Sugar is behind her.

"No, don't run." Sugar speaks, "Does it feel good, Celia? Do you feel how badly he wants you?"

Celia moans, and her arms get tighter around my neck.

Sugar continues behind her, holding her to me. "Touch him, Celia. Explore what's yours. You want her to do that, Judd? You want her to show you how much she wants you?"

"Fuck yes." I groan, pulling my lips from my wife, barely to get the words out.

Celia pushes her tongue further into my mouth, and we make out like horny teenagers for the first time.

Celia's hands shake, but she trails her fingers down my arms and then along my sides. All the while, Sugar is encouraging her like a sexy cheerleader.

"Judd, she's not porcelain. Give her more." Sugar grabs hold of my hand, holding onto Celia's waist, and tries to push it down to her ass. I don't budge. I'm grateful for whatever is going on here, but I'm not going to do anything that makes Celia uncomfortable.

I pull away slightly, and Celia is panting, her hands

pulling me back. I look again into her eyes, waiting for her response.

"More, oh please, Judd more."

"Fuck." I mutter before I drop my hands to her ass and squeeze her to me. The last threads of my restraint breaking away.

Celia

I've never done anything like this. It seems like Sugar is bringing more out of me than I thought possible. I'm so hot for Judd, but hearing Sugar in my ear makes it ten times hotter. She's barely touched me, but something about her presence just makes me want to lower all my walls.

Judd has never been anything more than soft with me, mostly because anytime he tried, I'd back away. Even the first time we had sex, it was romantic on a picnic blanket at the edge of the lake. He rocked me slow and kissed me tenderly. That was the time I got pregnant. Now just feeling him grip onto me as if he'll die if I move away is driving me wild. Sugar is right; there's nothing for me to be ashamed about. The more he hugs me, the more it makes me want to be bolder.

Judd tugs at my top, and I slip my hands under his shirt. His back arches as I rake my nails down his back.

"Oh fuck," He groans before he grabs hold of my hair, pulling the ribbon out and letting it drop to the floor. "You want this, Cel. You want me to fuck you rough."

"Yes," I say and wait. He doesn't seem to oppose it, but I

won't know until it's over. Right now, I'm just going to revel because he's giving me more than usual.

"That's what I want to hear, tell him." Sugar moans slightly, and Judd pulls his shirt off. Showing the both of us his gorgeous body. His years working outdoors have toughened him up; they've built muscle that most men can't get in the gym.

"Damn, babe, he's so gorgeous. I'm jealous." Sugar laughs slightly, then kisses my cheek before she steps away. I hear her taking a few steps in the door's direction. I guess she feels like since she already put us on the path that she's no longer needed. She may no longer be needed, but I don't want her to go.

"No, don't leave."

Both Judd and her stare at me. I look back over to Jud to get his approval. Time to put Sugar's theory to the test. "I want her to stay. Can she stay?"

Judd's head leans back, and a sinister smile crosses his face before he looks back at me, "I don't know what the fuck happened when I went to the store, but I love every second. If you want her to stay Cel, I want her to stay."

I clasp on to him, so ready to just drop on the bed and start rolling around, but I had to make sure that Sugar was okay. I want her to be comfortable. Even though she seems to be open to the idea of being with me and being with a man, I don't know if she's open to the idea of being with us, not like this. Not so soon.

"Stay?" I ask her.

She nods, and a kaleidoscope of butterflies erupts in my

gut. I can't believe she's going to stay. It's fast and foreign to me, but it feels so right.

"I want to watch you two first. I want to see you both truly break apart." Sugar says as she walks over to the patterned covered sitting chair and pulls it slightly closer to the bed before she sits and watches us.

"Seems we have an audience?" Judd says. He's in his element. I hate the fact that my hesitation and my chill kept the real him locked up all this time. This Judd turns me on. This Judd makes me want to do things I've never done before. Starting with putting on a show.

Sugar

This entire night is proof that the saying is true.

Some people only need a little push.

Celia was boiling at the surface, just desperate to be more than what all her exes made her believe she was. She only needed someone to convince her it was okay. She only needed someone to tell her that her needs aren't anything she needed to be ashamed of.

I'm glad it was me to push her along.

"Christ, Cel. I need you now." Judd growls out before he pulls her shirt over her head and flings it to the ground.

I'm used to being asked to be part of a threesome. Sometimes I indulge, but most time, I don't. I've always known that I wanted to be in a relationship that felt like a cacoon, a love that surrounds me. Being with more than one person isn't strange to me. The problem is, I've never met a couple or group where I fit in. Either the woman was jealous, the man just wanted to be selfish, or they were complete unto themselves.

Judd and Celia are different.

Sure, if I walked out of here right now, they would still have the time of their lives, but it feels like they want me here as much as I want to be here. They are focused on each other, but every once in a while, one of them will look over at me and make sure I'm okay. I'm over here, but they are still trying to keep me involved.

The space between the three of us crackles with sexual tension. It weighs heavily on my body.

"Tell him how you want it, sweetheart. I want to hear you. Please." I squeeze my thighs together tighter as I watch Judd yank Cel's pants off and spread her legs wide.

"Go in slow. I like to feel all of you. "

"Holy fuck. I feel like I died and went to heaven." Judd kicks his pants off, and I suck in a breath when I get a good look at his cock. He's thicker than I imagined he would be.

"Oh…mmm." I moan out, unable to keep myself silent. Every second I hear her panting and moaning for him, my need spirals further out of control. I don't want to fuck them tonight. I need to know that they want me there and I won't be a mistake tomorrow.

"Show her Judd. Sugar wants to see you. Can she?"

Celia is sexy as hell, sexier than I think she will ever know. Her sweet, sultry voice and that long silky brown hair give her an innocently slutty vibe. The type of girl you hear driving people wild simply by saying I'm a bad girl.

"Fuck, yes. She can see. Come here, Sugar. I want you to see what I have for my wife."

I don't want to get up, but his words tug on me as if they are wrapped around my neck like a rope. I unsteadily get to my feet and take the short few steps in his direction.

He turns slightly in my direction, and I watch him take himself in his hand, "You're so thick." I purr out. Before I turn my head to Celia, who is lying panting on the bed, waiting for him. Her eyes are glued to me, her pupils are wide and full of excitement.

"You run the show Celia, all the time." I remind her one more time. I don't want her to do anything that she's not comfortable with.

She nods but doesn't say anything.

I can feel my thighs dampen from how wet I am. My panties are still drying in the bathroom, so nothing is soaking up the juices coming from my pussy.

"Can I touch you?" I ask her.

"Yes, please." She replies coyly.

My eyes flip to Judd. This may be her show, but this is still his woman. "If she wants it, so do I." He repeats for me again. I take a step forward and grab hold of one of her legs and run my hand down her trembling thigh and to her apex.

Judd's eyes follow me every step of the way. When I use my pointer and thumb to spread her lips open, he whimpers.

"Judd, you're so thick. Her pussy is so tight. I don't know how you'll fit."

"Oh, God!" Celia's body shakes a little harder. "That's so sexy. Why is that so sexy?" She asks no one in particular.

"Because it's the truth. Your body is absolute perfection. I'm so wet just thinking about Judd pounding into you. You want that?"

"Now, Judd. God, fuck me now. I'm dying." Celia begs, and I have to squeeze my legs together harder. I'm going to come without either of them touching me.

I keep hold of Celia's leg and hold her pussy open while Judd slowly pushes himself into her. He snarls and curses as he dives in, her pussy sheathing himself to the base.

I'm not new to sex, but even though It wasn't me he was stretching out. I swear my body feels like someone had never fucked before me. I'm needy.

Celia whimpers and tries to pull away. I can feel her legs tensing up and then Judd tensing up right after her. They are so in tune with each other. I feel almost blessed that they let me into their little world. Blessed and challenged. Neither one of them wants to push the other more than they're used to, but sometimes good things come to those who try.

"Don't run, baby. He's not going to hurt you. It's going to feel so good, Celia. I promise you it will." I feel her relax, and Judd looks up at me with a sexy, lazy smile on his face.

He slowly pumps into her, and I feel Celia relax. Her hips are swerving up and down to meet his thrusts. My hips moving against nothing in the same motion.

I'm so damn hot right now. I move one of my hands off Celia and push it up the small shirt she gave me.

"Judd, she's hurting." Celia moans and tips her head back so she can see me.

"Off. Take 'em off", Judd grunts out through his steady thrusts into his wife.

I shouldn't do this, but I can't stop now. I kick off the ugly brown flats and yank down the black leggings to show the both of them my waxed and pierced pussy.

"Mmmm, you're beautiful. So beautiful." Celia whispers as she takes me in.

"Fuck, the top." Judd leans down and hooks his arms behind Celia's knees, making her scream out and her head arch off the bed. He focuses back on her.

"Don't stop Judd, fuck her." I pull my shirt off and stand to the side, watching as her glorious tits bounce up and down as he does exactly what I ask.

"Oh Judd, I'm coming. Oh... God!" Celia cries out, and my knees nearly buckle from the force of her orgasm.

"Shit, that's intense." I whimper. I want that. I need to come now. My hands roam over my body, but it's not enough.

I'm so focused on him thrusting into her I barely recognize when she pushes him away.

He moves immediately.

"It's too much?" Judd asks.

"No. Do you trust me, Judd?" Her voice is thready, like speaking is taking every ounce of energy.

"What? Yes, I trust you."

"Can I play with her? Will you be mad? I won't do it if you don't want me to."

"You're asking me if you can love on her while I'm loving on you?"

"Yes, is it okay to try?"

Judd doesn't say a word. He simply rakes his eyes over my body and stopping briefly at all the bruises that still liter my skin.

"I'm going crazy. I must have died." He leans down and kisses her gently. "Cel, if you want Sugar to be with us, I'm sure we have enough love to share."

My heart melts at the words. That's my dream to be with people that just want to love with no boundaries.

She smiles and turns around, kneeling on the bed. Her face is determined, and her smile is sweet, but I can tell she is nervous.

She wraps her arms around my neck. "I've never done anything like this before. You'll tell me if you don't like it?"

"I love it already, babe. You use me however you want." I rub my nose against hers and press our foreheads together. Her chin tips up slightly. She wants to kiss me but is holding back. I move the rest of the way and seal my lips over hers.

The deep ache I felt a few seconds ago intensifies, and I want to pull her away from Judd and just let her ride my face, but I think that might be too much for her.

She's full of passion, unbridled, and fresh.

"I can't believe this shit is happening," Judd says from behind us. I laugh and look over Celia's shoulder. He has his dick in his hand and seems to be mesmerized as his wife kisses me.

Celia angles herself on the bed, so she's in between the both of us. "Judd, I want more." She mutters before she gets on all fours and presses her backside in his direction.

"Mother-fucking hell. I'm not going to last long." Judd positions himself and pushes back inside his woman. I slide my hand to my pussy, but Celia surprises me by pulling on my legs until my slit is right by her face.

"Tell me if you don't like it." She whispers right before she tentatively sticks her tongue out and swipes it tenderly against my pussy.

"Oh shit! More, please." I move closer to her, and she does the same again, but this time with a bit more force behind it.

"Oh my god," Judd grunts out.

I lift one leg and prop it up on the bed, so I'm open for Celia. "Use your fingers, fuck my pussy the way Judd is fucking yours."

Celia gasps and pushes her face deep into my pussy, her tongue sliding and flicking at my opening.

I dig my hands into her hair and feel her hand rubbing against me. She uses two fingers to dip inside of me slowly; she moans loudly against my clit as her hands find the same rhythm as Judd.

"Oh fuck, Jesus. I need to fuck you harder. I need to get deeper." I watch him latch onto Celia's hips, his fingers digging into her skin, leaving red marks.

"Yes, Celia, like that. Oh, that feels so damn good." She pounds into me with her fingers the same way Judd fucks her with his cock. Her oral is a novice level, and a few times, she stops when she gets distracted by Judd, but she's still managed to bring me right to the peak.

"Cel, you're going to make me come. So fucking hard. I love you. Oh god." Judd throws his head back and really begins to pound into her. The violence of his thrust bumps her harder into my clit.

"Oh fuck yes! Yes. Fuck me, Celia. Yes!" I cry out as she sucks on my clit. My body clenches around her fingers, still deep in my cunt. She lets out a high-pitched squeal, and I feel her body tremor hard.

"Yes, she's coming. Can you feel her, Judd? Him, is she milking that cock?" I roll my hips against her face, my body still riding high from that earth shattering climax.

"Fuck yeah, Sugar, she's so tight. Oh fuck, I'm coming. I'm coming so fucking deep inside of you, Cel." He slams into her one final time before his body bows over forward, and he growls out his release. Just as he does, Celia sucks my clit again, and my knees give way. Judd's long-arm juts out and catches me just before I fall. He softly pushes me until I'm on the bed. Celia moves away from my pussy and trails tender kisses up my stomach and chest until she gets to my mouth, where she pecks me once before she rolls over and reaches for Judd.

He pulls her into his arms, and they lay there perfectly satisfied, at ease, and in love. I smile wide, happy I could help them achieve this even if my role took on a more significant part than I first expected.

I try to slide out of bed softly, so I don't disturb them, but Celia's hand reaches back and grabs hold of me.

"Where are you going?" She turns and mumbles sleepily.

"I'm just going to leave you two to have your private time. I don't need to horn in on that."

"Horn in? You're part of our private time. I meant it when

I said I want you to stay." She turns back to Judd, but this time she pulls me until my arm wraps around her waist. I expect Judd to look at me with some level of discontentment, but instead, he reaches over Celia and lays his hand on my hip in a possessive matter.

"Alright, I guess I can lay here for a little while," I reply just as sleepily. It's been a long time since I've felt this wanted. Why not bask in it a little bit.

15

Sugar

I wake up early the following day, still wrapped up in the two of them. Unfortunately, my body hurts, and I can't say it's from the mind-blowing sex that we had last night. The bruises and cuts I got from falling from my bike are far from healed, and my body is reminding me I need to take it easy.

I tiptoe into the bathroom and take a quick shower. The water pressure isn't very good, but it'll do. I put on the underwear I hand washed and step back into the leggings and small shirt Celia let me have.

I check the bag for the eyeliner I ask Judd to get and am surprised to see a small to-go makeup kit. It's all drugstore brand products, but it will do. I put on the eyeliner, mascara, and lip liner. I wish I had my earrings, but I already feel so much better with just this little change.

I don't know why Baxter can't see the girl he thought I was supposed to be is so different from who I really am.

I'll never be ashamed of how I look or how I love.

I look over at the couple that brought me with them into their small slice of heaven. I'm sure it's only a one-time thing, but I know it's one experience I'll remember for a long time. The both of them are so raw, so eager to please each other and all of that spilled onto me. I feel so damn lucky.

I softly walk out of the large B&B suite and make my way down the stairs. It's still pretty early, and I don't know if anyone else is awake or even if anyone else is here besides the owner.

Judd said there was a small library downstairs. Maybe I can sit there and wait for them to wake up. I need to contact the police ASAP and maybe meet up with Wire and the rest of the guys to get an escort back down to Eve's Fury. I know Baxter will never go up against a bunch of Wire's guys. He may be brave enough to go up against me, but never against another man. He's a wuss like that.

I turn into the small library and am surprised to see a small upright piano. A tear prickles the corner of my eye. Out of everything that I ever had with Baxter, I only miss the music. The way my fingers flew across the keys as I reached an intricate part in the piece excited me. I loved the happiness on the people's faces when they heard me play. Even the touring from place to place was fun for a while. The problems started when Baxter saw me as his ticket to the upper class.

He saw me as a way to break into the world of people his low-income family never fit into. Sure, the concerts and the touring left me with a nice sum of money, but I never wanted the life he was so desperate to give me. I just want to be happy and loved. That's all.

I walk over to the piano and pick up the cover. I let my hands fall on the keys, and the instant I press down, every note comes flooding back into my body, and I play like I never stopped.

The joy, pain, and fear roll through me as I play. Hiding this significant part of me is draining, and right now, it's more than I can take.

My fingers stumble for the first time, and a sob wracks my body. I put my face in my hands, and I cry. Why won't he just leave me alone? Why is it so hard to just be happy?

"Hey, hey, no, don't cry." A deep voice speaks before I feel someone sit on the bench in front of me and pull me into their chest.

It's Judd.

I pull away, "I'm sorry. I didn't mean to wake you." I wipe the tears off my face and try to smile at him.

"You don't have to hide from me, Sugar."

My head tilts slightly as my mind replays a déjà vu. Jag said something like this before all this crap went down.

"You don't need to be dealing with this." I sigh and look away.

"Sugar, I don't think I have ever seen Celia open up the way she has with you. I haven't known her very long, but I know that she's one of the best people I've ever met. She feels the same way about you. Something about the trauma the both of you share strengthens the connection that you both are building. If she's dealing with this, so am I." He rubs my arm.

"What are you saying?"

"I'm saying as long as you want us around, we'll both be around. Don't hide who you are from us because we want to see all of you."

The weight of those words slices straight through to my soul. How did I get so lucky to meet these two?

"Babe?" Celia comes down the stairs.

Judd and I are sitting close, and for most couples, it would be unacceptable. This arrangement the three of us have is more than just new it's premature. I still need to take my cues from the two of them since it's me who is squeezing into their space.

"Yeah?" Judd answers but doesn't move away. "Everything okay?"

"I don't think so. Sugar baby, I think you need to see this." Cel walks over to us and sits on the opposite side of me. She pulls up the phone she's holding and shows me a bulletin.

"Fuck! Fucking hell. What is this?" Judd barks and pushes his hands through his hair.

Sadness consumes me, and I have to cry again. This time instead of just Judd holding me, the both of them do.

My eyes don't leave the bold alert that was patched through to the phones in the area.

"Diana Elgin, 5ft9inches, white Hispanic female with jet

black hair reported abducted. The victim is mentally ill and needs help. If you see her, please call your local police department."

There goes my plans on getting the police involved. Of course, Baxter would go to them. According to him, I'm not in my right mind and need to be taken care of. No one ever listens to me when I say that I can take care of myself. Instead, they just keep sending me back to the man trying to break me down.

16

Sugar

After about of crying, I know what I need to do. Baxter will not stop, not until he has me back under his thumb. He won't be happy until there isn't a trace of Sugar left in me.

I can't just sit here and wait for him to show up. I definitely can't just sit by and watch Judd and Celia get dragged down in my mess.

I need to remember how strong I've become and get myself out of this mess.

"Okay, this is what's going to happen. We need to get out of here ASAP. If that message went out to everyone in the area, I'm sure the owner has seen it too. You two are going to drive back the way you came. Go straight to the cops and let them know what you saw.

I'm close enough to get up to Maine to get the help of a few of my friends. They can drive me back down to my clubhouse, and I can get this all worked out. We need to move fast. I don't want Baxter to close us in."

"You didn't listen to me earlier, I see." Judd glares at me, but I don't know what he's upset about.

"What are you talking about?"

"We're all in this together, Sugar. Why do you think we would just run away? What happens if Baxter cuts you off on your way to your friends, and you end up in the same position. What good does that do anything?" Celia is the one to answer, her anger visible as her lips press together tightly and her chest heaves up and down.

"This is crazy. You don't know me. You don't know my problems or anything about what I'm about. I could be a serial killer for all you know?"

"Do you kill people?" she asks curiously.

"Have you?" I ask her, ignoring her question.

"Yes," she answers right away. Both Judd and I look at her in shock. That's not what she's supposed to say. Who the fuck did she kill? Holy shit, there is so much more to Celia than it seems.

"What?" Judd asks, his voice low.

"They cleared me of the charges, but I killed a man named Riley Brant." She put her head down, not wanting to meet either mine or Judd's eyes.

"It doesn't matter. I don't want you guys in trouble like this. You've done so much for me already. You rescued me, clothed me, fed me, gave me one of the best nights of sex in my life." I smirk at them and grab Celia's hand. "Please don't put yourself in danger now. If something happens to you, I just don't know how I could ever forgive myself."

"How do you think we'd feel if something happens to you?" Judd shakes his head, "No, it's not happening, Sugar. We're with you until this is over. If you want to kick us to the curb after that, then you can do it. Until then, Baxter is going to have to get through both of us to get to you."

Celia nods her head once hard to show she's going right along with that plan.

"The both of you are crazy. You know that, right?"

In a rare moment, Celia shoots me a wink, "Crazy for you."

"Babe, you're so sexy." I pull her in and kiss her softly before I turn and do the same to Judd. His mouth is soft, and he quickly looks to Celia to make sure it's okay. So far, everything that we've done has been me with her.

She bites down hard on her lip before a sultry smile curl up her face. "We better get moving before I lock the three of us in a room, and we never come out."

"That sounds like an outstanding fucking plan," Judd says.

I shake my head as I rush back up the stairs to get our things and get on the road, hopefully with no surprises from Baxter.

17

Sugar

Wire, Roth, and a prospect named Brim catch up with us. I haven't seen anything of Baxter, but just having the three of them around to make sure nothing happens is really putting my mind at ease.

Judd drives us in the car as we follow the small group of bikes down to Eve's Fury. I sit in the back with Celia.

"Were you always like this? Outspoken, brave?" She plays with my hair.

"No, not at all. I mean, I always knew that I was a little different from everyone else, but I tried really hard to conform to what everyone wanted me to do. It's one reason I was with Baxter for so long. He was the right choice according to everyone else."

"Fucking douche hat." Judd grumbles.

I laugh and rub my fingers into his hair, scratching him softly. I turn back to Celia, who is wearing a big smile when I turn back around.

"What's that about?" I put a finger in the corner of her mouth and press on the little divot.

"You're really okay with this?"

"With what?" I wasn't understanding. Is she talking about Baxter?

"The two of us?"

"Oh." I glance to the rearview mirror and see that Judd is looking at me. Both of them are interested in my answer. "Well, I already told you I love love. I'm polyamorous, so being with over one person isn't a real shocker for me. The shocker is how quickly the two of you took to it. Usually, it takes years for any type of situation to come up. Even then, most of those arrangements don't work. I know the vow you two have together is sacred, and I'd never do anything to get in between that. I find you utterly breathtaking." I pick Celia's hand up and kiss her knuckles like they do in those cheesy movies. "Judd is handsome and strong willed." I rub his neck and he turns his face to kiss my fingertips. "All I want is to be happy, for you two to be happy. If you feel like I'm keeping you from completely being happy, I'll exit with no ill will or argument."

"What if we don't want you to leave?"

I feel my eyebrows cinch in as I try to understand what she's saying.

"Sugar, we talked about it this morning when the two of

us were in the shower. It may not be the most conventional way to have a relationship, but we both want to explore this. I thought Celia would feel some type of way or hell, even me. I'm not used to sharing, but to see her happy, see her so free and at ease like she was last night is more than I can ask for." Judd says from the front seat.

"Yeah, and I can tell Judd feels more relaxed when you are there. I feel more powerful when you're around. You make me feel like it's normal to be this way. Normal that I like women and men. Normal that I want to watch Judd and you make love before he turns to me and takes me. Everything that everyone else told me was wrong or made me a whore you've already shown me is perfect for who I am. I don't want you to go. I want you to stay with us." Celia caresses my cheek before she leans in and kisses me.

I grab the back of her head and deepen the kiss, she doesn't pull away like she used to with Baxter instead she moans into my mouth and I swallow it down.

"Girls, don't make me pull over." Judd warns us from the front.

"What'll happen if you do? It sounds like a threat, Judd. I think the two of us can take you." I laugh.

"Fucking hell, the both of you can take me anytime you want."

"Holy shit, are they making out back there?" Brim was on the side of the car and is looking in as Celia and I continued to make out.

I hear Judd roll down the window and scream out. "Hey, Fuck off!"

"Lucky, selfish bastard!" The prospect retorts and I laugh. Yeah, this is going to be fun.

* * *

WE STOP ONCE to fill up and grab a few quick things to eat. We've been driving for longer than 12 hours. Wire and his boys are still good, drinking red bulls and coffee's but Judd and Celia are burnt out. I take over driving just so we don't have to pull into a motel. Sooner or later, we will.

"Hey boo, you boys need anything?" I walk up to Brim. "No, I'm okay. You might want to check Wire and Roth, they haven't been able to get into the store yet. He motions with his head toward a sitting tractor trailer. I hope they weren't back there taking a leak.

I follow the sound of voices until I find where they are.

"Roth, I don't give a fuck what happened in the past. You can 't keep doing this to yourself. Pushing yourself like this. You asked to be a part of something good, to have one more shot at making a difference, but you not going to do no good like this. For fucks sake, why don't you listen.

"Wire, you don't understand. I don't have time, not for all the people I know still need the fucking help. I don't have time to relax. I don't deserve a rest, not after all the shit I've done." Roth shakes his head and leans against the hard steel.

Again I can see it. The man looks like he might fall over at any second. What is he looking for so hard?

"So what the fuck does that mean for me? I've done my

share of fucked up shit. Do you wish the same shit on me?"

"You're good far outweighs mine. You and I both- "Roth stops talking when he opens his eyes and sees me standing there.

Wire turns around fast, "What the fuck are you doing sneaking up on us, Sugar?"

"I wasn't trying to sneak up on you, babe, just wanting to know if you got everything you need for the last leg? Drinks? Food?"

"We're fine." Wire looks at Roth once more before he shakes his head and walks away.

Roth tries to do the same but I stand in front of him, stopping him. "You know you broke Vexx's heart?"

"Fucking hell. Sugar, I can't do this right now."

I put a hand up to stop him. "Roth, I don't know what's eating you, but I see it. Whatever it is, will eat at you until there's nothing of you left. It's a poison." I pull him into a hug, "Thank you."

"Thank you? What're you thanking me for?" He tries to pull away, but I don't let him.

"This poison will never let you make Vexx happy. She deserves to be happy. I'm guessing you know that. You leaving is her chance to find true happiness even if right now it feels like hell for her."

He sighs and hugs me back. "It's my only wish. I want nothing else for myself than for her to be happy. Thank you for understanding."

"Oh babe." I push off and start walking back, "That's what I do."

18

Sugar

After pulling off into a truck stop for a few hours letting Wire and his boys get some sleep, we finally make it back to familiar territory.

"There is a lot of wooded area around here." Judd says.

"Yeah. Our clubhouse is deep in the woods, on about 10 acres, if I'm not mistaken. We have done little with it though." I can't wait until I get back to the girls. I have been keeping in contact with Vexx and they have been able to work out getting Tori and Jag out of jail. Press hasn't been so lucky. His prints pulled up some cases that they want to look into so he's going to be in there for a while.

I'm sure Duchess isn't happy about that in the least.

"Have you seen anything else on the phone about me?" I ask Judd, who is sitting in the front driving again.

"No, no new alerts. That's good right?" He chances a glance at me.

"Yeah, I guess that means the cops stopped looking." I shrug but look out the window.

"That doesn't mean that Baxter did." Celia shivers and looks out the window.

"No, I don't think so." I turn away and look out my window. An eerie feeling creeps up my spine. Baxter's close, I just know it.

"Oh, my god! You fucking bitch! I could kill you! I'm missed you so much." Bee runs out the clubhouse and collides into me. I hiss out in pain and she lets go immediately.

"Aww, babe. It's nice to be back." I say as the tears come running down my face. We made it home with the help of Wire and his nomads. Roth didn't stay around. The second that Vexx saw him ride off, her face went stone hard. It's going to take us a long time to get over him leaving her.

The rest of the club comes over to me and they all engulf me in love. My entire soul is smiling by the time they are through.

"Uh, so who are these two?" Addison asks. She transfers Glenn from one hip to the next.

This is Celia and Judd. They saved my life and we're together."

"Together?" Riot asks, "How in the fuck? I mean, how you mean?" She scrunches her nose and looks between the three of us.

"I mean, I'm with both Celia and Judd."

"Oh, you lucky son of a bitch." Treble says from where he's standing next to Riot.

They all laugh, and Judd pulls me back to kiss me. I lean back and accept his affection.

"Oh crap, I need my bag." Celia bounces away and rushes over to the car to pull her bag out of the trunk.

Happiness turns to complete panic the second the first scream echos in the air.

"Judd! Oh god!"

"Celia!" I scream and run in her direction, Judd and everyone else behind me.

My head pounds and my mouth goes dry as I look into the woman who was just laughing and playing with me, pale in fear.

He was in the fucking trunk. The sly piece of shit hid in the trunk. Baxter's eyes are wild as he presses the gun against Celia's head.

"Let her the fuck go!" Judd roars and takes a step forward. Jag, Treble and Free behind him.

"Baxter, you don't want her, you want me. Let her go." I take a step myself, trying to cut them all off. I don't want him to get freaked out and shoot her. Addison has the baby out here. This can go bad real fast.

"I did, but I heard you. I followed all of you to the fucking rest stop and I heard the three of you fucking like wild monkeys in the room. You fucking whore! How could you defile yourself like that?You'll never do Diana. We could have had everything! I gave you everything! But you couldn't just sacrifice once for me."

"No, baby, I'm not going to sacrifice. Not my happiness, not who I really am. I don't want what you want to give me. I don't want you to take care of me. I just want to be who I am. She will not be who you want her to be so let her go."

"No! I'm not going to let her go. She's fucking staying with me!"

I see a bit of movement in the trees on the right of him but he's so busy looking at us he doesn't notice it. Everyone is behind me, so who can be in the trees?

"Hey, you piece of shit." Roth surprises him and runs toward him causing Baxter to swing the gun in his direction. The silencer is still on so I don't hear the pop, but I see the impact as it cuts into Roth's abdomen.

"No!" Vexx roars and rushes him, tackling the stunned Baxter to the ground and pushing Celia out of the way. Vexx takes out her weapon and at the same moment, everyone that is armed pulls their weapons ready to kill, but Wire rolls up. "No! Put the guns away. Don't fucking shoot! The cops are on the way!" He calls out.

My eyes dart to the dirt road behind him and I see two cars with flashing red and blue lights.

Fuck, they finally caught up with him. Or maybe they caught up with me?

19

Judd

The cops pull up shortly after Roth jumped out to help. I didn't even know they had turned back. Apparently, Wire caught wind of the cops pulling up and wanted to warn Sugar. Celia is shaken, but she's refusing to go to the hospital.

"Judd, I promise I'm fine."

"Bullshit, you had a gun to your head. It was shot near your ear. You need to get checked out."

"Ma'am if you want to do that, now is the time." The police officer that took our statement says.

"No, I promise. I'm fine. It was just a scare, but now that you have that bastard in custody, we can go on about our lives." She smiles at the man, then turns back to me. The officer nods his head and walks over to where his other officers' buddies are. All of them talking to the eve's fury women. Talking to Wire. Roth and Vexx were rushed to the hospital, but besides the small patch of blood on the floor, you wouldn't even be able to tell a madman had just run through and tried to kill my wife or my new girlfriend.

I try not to be an asshole and smile at that thought, but I can't help it.

I was resolved to being in a forever marriage with Celia. I love her, she's gorgeous and I know she'll be faithful. Sure, I was struggling with how closed off she was. I would have stayed with her. I would have made it work.

Talk about turning my world upside down. Not only has she bloomed basically overnight but now I have two women to care for, two women who care for me. Two women who want to please me. I can't wait.

"What are you thinking about?" Celia knocks me out of my daydream.

"I'm thinking about what I'm going to have to do to find a job around here?" I pull her into my chest and kiss away all my worries. I trust her. If she says she's good than she is.

"Oh, I'm going to have to get used to that. I think I might like people looking a bit more than I thought." Celia purrs and nuzzles me.

"I'm here to please. We can give them a show if you want." I smile.

"Nah, our only shows are for Sugar." Celia rubs my arms.

"Hmm, you got to love an interactive audience."

Celia laughs and I walk her into the clubhouse to look for our other women.

***

Sugar

The cops came in and after everyone explained Baxter stowed away in my car to find me and try to kill me, they finally believed me. They hauled him away in handcuffs and I feel bad for him as they drove off.

Now there are a few other police officers here asking questions. I'm so glad Wire had the thought to ride back and tell us what was going on because it was about to be a full-blown firing squad if he didn't say anything. That means more people in jail, more families separated.

"Babe, you okay?" Celia walks over to me and wraps her arms around my waist.

"Yeah, I'm just happy all this is over. You both still have the option to turn around and leave. My life is nothing but crazy."

"Nah, you're stuck with us. Where is your room?" Celia asks, and I point to my space. It's small and won't be very comfortable for the three of us, but for right now, it'll do.

Judd walks up behind me and swats my ass playfully before he follows Celia into the room. Oh, I can't wait until we can all really relax. I'm needing more of the both of them.

I look around the clubhouse to see if there's anything changed and realize I don't hear Glenn crying. Maybe he's finally over his bout of colic.

I knock on Addison's room, but I hear nothing.

I look out the window that shows the front, but I don't see her out there either. I walk back over to her room and knock again.

No answer.

Oh god, where's the baby? A million horrible thought run through my head when I open her bedroom door and don't see neither Addison or Glenn. All their stuff is here but there gone.

"Oh no. Glenn! Addison! Addy!" I yell and I hear a soft whine.

Glenn's crying. I look under the bed and out the door. I know I heard it coming from in here. I hear it again and it sounds like it's coming from the closet.

"Addison, you in there?" I open the door and see both Addison and Glenn deep in the closet's corner.

"What are you doing? Everything is over, baby." I put my hand out and try to coax her out.

"I can't go out there, he can't see us."

"Honey, Baxter is gone. He can't hurt us anymore." I didn't realize she was so scared of Baxter. She seemed fine when they put him in the patrol car.

"No, not Baxter. The cops."

"Why not? You didn't do anything wrong, honey." I soothe.

"He'll take Glenn. I didn't think I'd ever see him again."

My heart beats double time. "Why? Who?"

"The cop. The young one with the gray hair. That's Glenn's father."

My mouth drops open. We all knew that Glenn's father

was some crooked cop, but we never expected to see him here. Not in our own backyard.

We had to keep her away from him at all costs, but how the fuck do we go up against the police department.

EPILOGUE

Hardy

What the fuck. I know that girl.

It's a fucking mad house the second we all get on the scene. We get the one crazed perp into the squad car with no further gun fire.

Baxter shot one of the civilians, but it looked like he was going to pull through.

We've been chasing this woman, Diana Elgin, the famous concert pianist through the state because her ex told everyone she wasn't of sound mind and the people she was with kidnapped her. Turns out the ex is the one we should have been taking to jail. Not only did he have a weapon with a silencer, but he had about 3 grams of meth in his pocket. He was high out of his mind.

I should have agreed to go back to the station with him, but instead I decided to stay around and get statements.

As a rookie, it's better to just get the shit jobs over with than have to be told.

A small girl with messy hair and a petite stature runs into the large compound. Since we don't have a warrant, the members of this so-called club won't let me in. I don't know what they're hiding in there, but I know that girl.

Even though I'd give my right nut sack if it wasn't truly her, I can't deny what I saw. She was my worse mistake. The one choice that let me know not even the good guys had my back. That's the woman who can end my career before it starts and put me in jail for a fuck ton of years. Not only that, but she was holding a baby.

A baby that looks to be just the right age to be mine

MORE FROM RAE B. LAKE

<u>Wings of Diablo MC</u>
Wire
Archer
Clean
Cherry
Prez
Ryder
Ink
Roth
Mack
Storm
Dillon
Pope
Treble

<u>Wings Of Diablo MC - New Orleans</u>

Jameson

Yang

Bones

Spawns of Chaos MC

Shepard

Tex

Maino

Juric Crime Family

Sven's Mark

Josip's Secret

Kaja's Bet

Eve's Fury MC

Becoming Vexx

Free

Riot

Duchess

Sugar

Dark Duet

His Darkest Needs

Her Darkest Gift

Boys of Djinn MC

Wyatt

(Wyatt, Book 1 is in the Twisted Steel Anthology)

Cody

The Shop Series Books
His Georgia Peach
To Protect and Serve Donut Holes
On The Edge of Ecstasy
His Peach Sparkle

Royal Bastards MC
Death & Paradise
Chaos & Paradise

Standalones
Drunk Love
Saving Valentine

FOLLOW RAE EVERYWHERE!

FACEBOOK

READER GROUP

TWITTER

INSTAGRAM

GOODREADS

AMAZON

WEBSITE

BOOKBUB

NEWSLETTER

TIKTOK

RAE'S ON KINDLE VELLA!

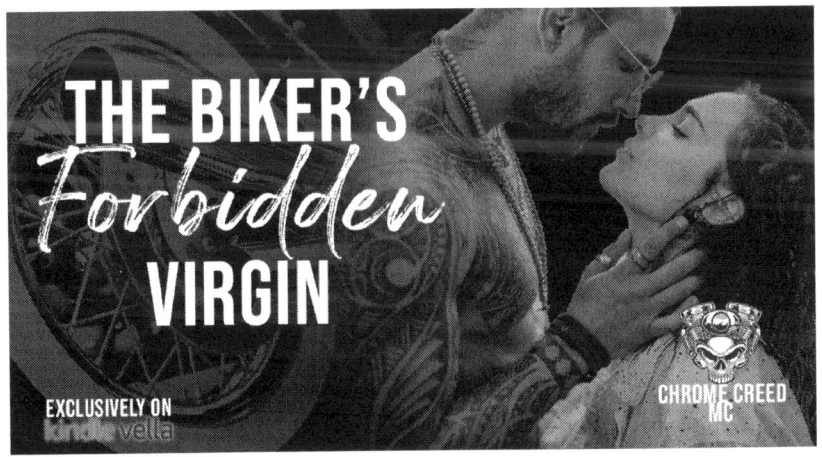

I'm the President of the Chrome Creed MC. A position that comes with privileges. I've never been an easy man, nothing about me soft or slow. I take what I want, hard and fast, until I'm through. Holding back is not something I do until I set my eyes on Nisa. She's young, pure, and not meant for a man like me. Something about her calls to the beast inside me, pushing me past the point of control. I warned her, but she didn't listen. She's completely off-limits. Forbidden. Now she's all mine.

Read it here!

Made in the USA
Middletown, DE
09 October 2021